I0540830

BLACK
BLOOD
EARTH

BENJAMIN DeHAAN

JOURNALSTONE
YOUR LINK TO ARTIST TALENT

ISBN: 978-1-68510-150-3 (trade paper)
ISBN: 978-1-68510-151-0 (ebook)
Library of Congress Catalog Number: 2025932706

First printing edition: March 14, 2025
Printed by JournalStone Publishing in the United States of America.
Cover Artwork and Interior Map: Mikio Murakami
Edited by Sean Leonard
Proofreading, Cover Layout, & Interior Layout by Scarlett R. Algee

JournalStone Publishing
1400 North Wood Rd.
Murphysboro, IL 62966

JournalStone books may be ordered through booksellers or by contacting:
or
JournalStone | www.journalstone.com

For little Ema.

Poranda

BADVAL SEA

GORGAD SEA

RUST PIRATE TERRITORY

GLACIER FIELDS

MT. GRAY

THE SHARD

CAVES

LAKE BLUESMERE

BOULDER LANDS

FISHRAT VILLAGE

FRADSHIQ BAY

HOTATA ROOT FIELDS

FORLORDA FORTRESS

LEKKA RIDGE

HULAND SANDS

BADGAL VILLAGE

TRUSS SEA

UNCHARTED

UNCHARTED

UNCHARTED

N
W E
S

BLACK

BLOOD

EARTH

CHAPTER 1
SHADOWS IN THE NIGHT

I'm half asleep when the visions of Sara come to me again in the cold of night. I toss about, ignore the sharp stabbing of cullet grass stuffing in my bed, and bury my face into the pillow.

No matter how hard and tight I pull the rigid sheep hide over my head, the screams remain sharp and penetrating, always coming firm and thick through our frosted hut, our little home in Bangal Village.

My mind goes quiet save the sound of freezing valley wind playing amongst tree branches and snow showering against the outer walls. It's going to be a long, cold night. The nights are always long.

I push away the animal hide, which is like lifting a heavy piece of wood, and feel my way to my feet, balancing myself on the muddy walls. I squint at the crescent moon through the eyehole the size of a silver coin and see that the sheep shack is sound and quiet under moonlight. Save the visions and dreams, everything will be all right in Poranda if the sheep are undisturbed. The winter has even the Gorg wolf beasts sleeping deep in their dens. I sigh in relief and turn around. I want to return to my warm bed.

But there is a silhouette of a person in the doorway to Sara's room. My eyes adjust to the darkness and I see it's a girl. It's her.

"Father?" she says and comes close. Her face is wet and her short brown hair is mangled and dusted from the floor. She is a roller in her sleep, but the dirt can't hide her orange freckles, can't hide her cuteness. She falls into my body and hugs me around the waist. "You were yelling, Father."

"No, you were screaming," I tell her, but she shakes her head. I touch her cheek with a finger. "Your face is wet. You were crying."

"Yes, I cried. But I wasn't screaming. I cry quiet."

"Where did those tears come from?"

She looks up into my eyes, her chin resting on my belly button.

"You were yelling. So many times. I thought you were mad. Maybe mad at me."

"Never," I tell her. I put my weathered farmer hands on her soft plump cheeks and turn her into a fish that looks to be gasping for air. "You are the last thing on the Poranda continent I would be angry with."

She smiles and then begins to shiver. Her teeth chatter. The goatskin clothing isn't enough for this year's harsh winter, but there is not enough Halmic coin in the ground safe to thicken the clothing on our skin. Even the sheep that huddle in their pen are barer than the surrounding knolls. Warmth is like an unobtainable dream that floats further away the more you reach out and try to grasp it.

"Here, let me pick you up." I begin to wrap the goat skin around her body, but she tugs it away.

"I'm a big girl. I can make it to bed myself, Pa."

"I'm sure you can." I pet her head, but she turns away to go back to her room. "I know."

She disappears into the darkness where moonlight does not touch. She is growing. I need to give her more space, that much is true. But I want to be there for her always. Her parents are gone and I have taken her in. I worry that maybe they look down upon me now from above and grow disappointed I can't bring a fulfilling, deserving life to a child that works so hard and makes the best out of a healing world.

I go back to bed and lay down. I look up into the ceiling and imagine I'm floating through the cosmos and stars streak across my temples and dissipate into a black void behind me.

But no matter how many times I try to disappear into the black canvas behind my eyelids, rock and earth and boulders flare across my mind. I don't know where this landscape exists in my mind that sprawls and extends deep into the horizon.

Hills spread farther than the eye can see and great stone structures spread across unfertile land. Among the pillars that pepper the dark brown splash of paint that make up lolling lands, there is one structure that has caught my eye in the visions I see.

A great boulder the size of six of my huts combined floats midair and casts a great shadow upon something that sways below. I think I have seen this dream before. I have seen the children gathering in fields among a great giant rock just like this one.

But I have never seen it this clear, this vivid. I have never seen the girl that grits her teeth under the great boulder that is hovering high in my dream.

Both her hands are up and she waves them and trembles back and forth on her feet. It is clear that whoever it is is a female. She has brown hair. Her height is short and she doesn't have the rigid texture of a man. She screams up at the rock and it floats higher up into the air.

Her face is of confidence until the rock begins to float down again. Her legs dig hard into the ground and half of her foot is now buried underneath the soil. The boulder keeps coming, closing the gap between each other.

The face is pretty, yet strong on the one that tries to control such mass. Robed people slowly come forth into my vision and surround the girl that barely keeps the rock in control.

They nod at each other and the only green-robed being comes forth with a pillow. Set upon it is some kind of metal contraption. A tube filled with documentation. "The way to the past," the green-robed one says.

The girl screams and the rock splits and shatters into shards that spray the area below. The scream comes again and those rocks are further split and pulverized.

Screams come one after the other. It's Sara's voice!

"Father Milan!" Sara cries, and I roll out of bed in despair.

"Sara!"

I get up, but I am pushed down and slapped with metal across the cheek. It stings so bad I can barely open my eyes.

"Come on, that was too much," a voice says from the corner of the room as I wiggle my tongue around the wound inside my mouth. "You aren't getting coin to kill."

Two men in black cloaks grab me by the arms and pull me up out of bed and to my feet. My head swims and I sway back and forth like a drunk.

I am tugged and dragged, the tops of my feet scraping along the floor as the men make their way across the room. A third man shuffles behind me but does not put a hand to me.

"Easy with him now," the old man's voice comes. He huffs and puffs as if struggling to keep up. "I want him ready and fit."

"Ready and fit?" The man pulling hardest on my arm scoffs. "He is scrawny and probably couldn't crack a loaf of bread."

My daze begins to fade and I find strength in my mouth again. "What are you doing with me?" I yell, and toss about, but I can't shake the hard grips on my arm. We enter Sara's room but she is gone. Only her blanket of wool from last season remains in the middle of the mud room. Her shelves are broken about on the floor and story parchments are scattered as if a storm has come through. "What have you done with her?"

"You have done this to yourself," one of the men says, and ties my hands behind my back with rope. "Stealing other people's domestic animals! Atrocious, you are!"

The man on my right laughs and accidentally steps on my foot, nearly cracking the bone in one of my toes. I headbutt him in the neck and he flies to the ground. I catch the other man with an elbow across the chin.

I am about to turn when something clamps around my waist and I am totally unable to move. I can't move my head, nor my neck or back. I can still control my eyes, and I move them down to look at the contraption snug tight to my middle but there is simply nothing there. Nothing is pressed up against me. My legs stiffen and my heart races.

"Grab him tightly now, boys," the voice like gravel comes again. The same voice I heard back in my room. "Or I'll have all the coin back and make you both sleep in the Morg wolf caves!"

The men stumble back to their feet and this time wrap their arms under my armpits. They jerk me forward and my feet begin to grind again along the hard coarse dirt.

We burst out into the snowstorm that is like a wild animal in itself. I squint and try to see far into the horizon but still, Sara is nowhere to be found. I bite my tongue and want to choke myself to death for not being able to protect her.

I adopted her. I am the one responsible to keep her safe from the evil in this world. How weak I am, I think as my thoughts are pulled to my feet that sting now with freeze. They're dragged through thick snow down the knoll and I can barely keep my eyes open in the wind.

We continue down the dirt path down into the main part of town. There is no light in the other mud shacks. But through the great sheets of snow blowing ahead I make out a faint light. It is Bangal Village's town hall, a rock-stacked cylinder with a flat roof made from Para tree bark. In one of the windows there is a candle flickering.

The door flings open and Polo the townkeeper looks at me, gives a great sigh, and begins to shake his head as he leans against the door frame. "Bring him in, boys. You know where to take him."

"Polo, please," I say, and fold my hands together. "I have done nothing. I beg you... My girl..."

"That's what they all say. Done nothing. I'm sure you'll be able to think about what you've done long and hard by yourself," he says, and juts his thumb across the room. "In there!"

"But my daughter."

"Enough already. Boys?"

The two men swing me like a wild dog's chew toy into the enclosure and a great barred door booms shut.

Somewhere, out there, Sara is alone, taken, or maybe something worse has happened to her.

I bang on the barred doors and scream, but the candle has been blown out and no one remains. "My daughter!"

I begin to cough violently and it feels as if I've swallowed a handful of sharp rocks. My nerves are on fire, but it's cold, and I can barely keep my head from vibrating against the metal bars.

My old curse is back, I think, and pull my hand away.

I can't see it but I know it's there, running down my wrist, wet and warm.

CHAPTER 2
THE WEIRD ONE

I wake up with my forehead wedged in between two cold bars of metal. The morning light coming through the window stings my crusted eyes. Pain in my forehead lingers when I pull away from the door, and it's then that I realize I must have passed out during my coughing fit.

The blood that had come forth hot is now half dry and sticky on my hands, and no matter how hard I wipe it on my wool garments it clings with persistence.

I remember Sara and how I never saw her in her room and like a bolt of lightning to my heart I pull myself up to the metal bars. I begin to pound, kick, and yell, but I only bruise my body and become even more fatigued than when I had woken. I lean back against the rock wall and fall to the mud floor. The itch in my throat tells me I need to take it easy or I'm going to stir up another storm.

I've had whatever this curse is since my young years working in the Hotata root fields north of Bangal Village. It is a staple food in the southeast. The only problem is that the fields are too far to the north, too close to the place where the world ended once centuries ago. They grow deep into the ground, about the length of two full-grown men, and suck up an invisible poison from the old war, so they say, but it doesn't stop this village or the surrounding ones from eating it. It's all we have save about one sheep per year as we need the fury beasts alive to borrow their warmth.

Speaking of the sheep. I don't know how I could be blamed for the stolen animals. I have told Polo on many occasions that I keep to my own flock and that I can support myself on what I have built over the years across my little stretch of soil. I thought Polo trusted me. How could he put the blame on me? How could he? How could he, god damn it to the gods from above?!

The men pulled me from my bed, then I saw that someone or something had taken my daughter. I promised her mother of festering disease that I would take care of her until she could make it her by herself.

I lean back and the wall of stacked rocks stabs into my back.

Oh, I see you want to play with me, I think as I stare at the wall, as I understand that I have been stripped clean and I am bare to the fullest and I have no Sara and I no longer have a promise I can fulfill to her mother.

I pick up one rock after the other and lodge them into the wall, heaving and spitting and blowing blood through my nose. The cough comes and I could care less. I put in my work in the root fields and this is what has come of it. So be it. I have fed my daughter through it all and that is all that matters. That she is okay is all that matters.

And now I think...as I weep. Oh god of might, as I weep into my stained farmer hands and can't even feel the wetness from my own tears due to the decade-old calluses that no longer allow any feeling through my skin, I want to have my daughter back.

Please bring her back, someone, anyone, please.

"Surely, a thief should not be allowed to have their daughter back," a voice pierces the cold rock walls and the room is as empty as before. There is no one, but the voice comes again, a gravel voice that I slightly recognize but nothing comes to mind. It is just old and tired and not ready for anything that requires energy.

"You have done something that is not acceptable in these parts." I hear scraping of sand and dirt as if feet drag, but I see nothing. "You shouldn't have stolen poor old Draxen's stock. Pretty sick, if you ask me, since the whole lot of you are all starving. Pretty sick indeed. No, disgusting."

"I have done nothing!" I yell back. "Where is my daughter? Where is she?"

The voice comes again. "Settle down and then we can talk."

I get up and slam a wooden tray on the bars and it cracks in half. I take the two halves and toss them down the corridor. Surely, whoever was talking would be surprised by the flying objects and have no other choice than to come out from hiding. But the longer I wait, the quieter it gets, and there is no way that the person in hiding is going to come out, and no way I'm going to get out of this nasty-smelling cell.

"Settled?" the aged voice says and I whip myself around. There with me, sitting on the ground in the cell, is an old man whose face is like a baking brown raisin sticking forth from a spoiled thick white desert garment. The rest of his body is covered with the same dirtied attire. He sits cross-legged, a sandaled foot jutting out from both sides, and his hands are folded neatly between his crotch.

"Who are you?" I ask and pull my muddy wool sweater to my neck. I want to hide from this old man. He is obviously not of this world, this much is clear, as he just pops up wherever he pleases.

He yawns, oblivious to his own trickery. He takes a flask out, mumbles something about a desert, and takes in great gulps. A belch triggers his next action and he takes out an apple from within his robe and bites into it with a snap. He chews more loudly than my flock of sheep at morning meal.

"Milan, is it?" he says, and throws the core at my feet. He slowly rises and begins to walk back and forth in the back of the cell. "You are probably wondering why I am here."

I couldn't care less about the sudden appearance of this old man. I kick the apple core back at him and it rolls into a black pebble and stops at the tip of his sandal. He looks up and smiles, his pearly white teeth in bright contrast against his brown leather face. His old eyes widen to reveal their foggy film.

I have grown tired of being played with and I try to hold the boil inside at bay and settle my vibrating body against the cold metal bars.

"Where is Sara?"

"She has been taken."

"To where?"

"Far away."

"And where is far away?"

"I cannot tell you just yet. You have to make a promise to Sharp Eye."

"Who the hell is that?"

He twirls a finger at his face and gives a great sigh as if I was supposed to know that and continues to pace the room, scratching at his white beard.

"You have one choice, my boy. Only one. And that is to come with me. A four-day journey east."

Besides the Hotata root fields in the north, there is very little I know outside of Bangal Village. There are dangers out there that the old wars have given birth to. Creatures of unimaginable tenacity to kill and mountains that are alive, decimating, and cruel to the lands that surround them. I've even heard of a black slime virus that spreads through the earth and causes whole towns to collapse and burn.

I don't understand how this journey will bring me any closer to Sara. I only need to know where she is. I don't need this old man playing with my head.

"Enough is enough," I say. "Please just tell me where my daughter is!"

Sharp Eye rolls his eyes. "Like I said, a four-day journey east."

"Let's go right away then." I try to open the bars on the cell. "Let's get out of here, old man. What the hell are we waiting here for?" I turn back to him and wave a hand at the cell but he shakes his head and cracks an ugly grin.

"Not so fast. You have to make a promise."

"What is that?"

"I have paid coin to Polo to look after your sheep and make sure no one loots your little mud hut. I have made sure that you will have everything once your journey is finished. There will be nothing to worry about here. Trust me."

He approaches me and rips me forward with strong hands and clamps me hard into position so that his face is but a nose-length from my own. "Trust me," he continues. "All our worries are to the northeast. We must go. In return for your promise, in return to swearing allegiance to my lord and serving him until your duties are fulfilled, I promise to have your daughter back in your arms. You must promise you will serve him until your duties are fulfilled. Promise me!"

I pull my hands from his grasp. He is too close for comfort and I lean against the door that keeps me caged in here like a cornered field rat.

"Who took her? Your lord? Who, goddamn it, who?"

The old man puts a finger on his lips to tell me to shut up. There is a clicking noise from behind me, the door opens, and I fall to the ground outside of the jail cell. I look up at him as he towers above me like some insane storyteller of the southern volcano region that has had too much cave trickle juice.

He taps the metal bars with a knuckle. "Well, would you like to stay here?"

I shake my head in silence.

"Thought so."

CHAPTER 3
SICK IN THE SAND

We leave snowy Bangal Village and I am almost shocked how the climate has changed over the period of just two days. The air has dried and the snowy slush we had trudged through fades into dried, cracked earth that appears lifeless.

The temperature has risen so much I have relieved myself of most of my attire. But for some reason, Sharp Eye seems fine with his heavy white cloak. I wonder if the old man will pass out, but he walks ahead strong, and the lack of noise from his mouth indicates he is far from fatigued.

I'm agitated. No food or water for what has seemed like weeks. I catch up to Sharp Eye, who is making better pace than me along the parched earth floor. I grab him by the arm and turn him around. I am about dead now as we walk. I need at least some acknowledgment that we are not in the gravest of situations and need aid beyond our reach.

He slaps my hand away. "Now is not the time."

"I want water, I want my daughter, and I want assurance that you can take me to her. I can't just go..."

He throws me to the ground and lets out a great sigh as if he has lost all the air in his lungs.

"I'm not sure of this, I'm not sure of that. Just shut up and follow me. We are entering—"

But before he can finish his sentence, the first attack during our journey comes like a flash of lightning that doesn't give a coin if it kills its target.

Beasts abound in numbers I can barely keep tally. Just only on the second day of our travels, we've come across drooling mutated dogs that want to make a meal out of us.

They are a compound of brown, green, and purple, and their skin looks burnt as if they have been subjected to flame over many years without enough time to heal and recover from their injuries.

"Their vision is worthless," Sharp eye says. "Do not move a muscle."

I look to him and he is calm like a statue. How can he be so still whilst slobbering fiends walk left and right sniffing the ground before us? They seem to be looking for meat in the cracks of the desert, but it is clear when the multiple pair of eyeballs slowly rise from the ground, the only meat they are interested is the meat on our bones.

"I will be calm," I whisper to the crazy man, the weird one who has brought me on this great escapade. The beasts circle us, drool, and yelp to one another, most likely asking each other where their meal has disappeared to.

I feel something move across my feet below but I keep still. Tiny legs move quickly along my skin and the sensation slowly makes its way up my leg. I want to look down but I'm afraid of the beasts' gaping mouths in front of us.

"Do not even move a finger," Sharp Eye says, his voice slow and grave. "Do not even move an eyeball if you can."

But I look down and see a centipede-like tail longer than my arm disappear up into my pants. I feel a great pinch and stab on my inner thigh and give out a cry. I swat at the creature and crunch and twist it as best I can. It slithers out and I crush its head with the bottom of my sandal.

"Fool!" Sharp Eye yells, and the mutant dogs begin to yelp and cry and they enclose on us. It's over. Dinner is ready to be served. "Why weren't you still?"

"I was still!" I lie in shame.

I begin to sway back and forth and my mind grows foggy.

Sharp Eye pulls up the leg of my pants. "Oh, the devil. A sandbiter got you!"

Now it's all voices and growls and the heat from the sun above as my vision blackens. I fall to the ground and try to control my breath.

I wait for the bite to my neck. I wait for the life-ending crush and my blood to leave this body and feed the dry desert. I see Sara in my mind, making her way through life strong as ever and creating a great world for everyone in Bangal Village. Maybe she will be townkeeper someday, I think.

This is it.

Goodbye, Sara.

Stay…strong.

Sharp Eye shouts at the top of his lungs and I hear cracks so loud I wonder if trees fall in the unknown distance before me. The beasts yelp as Sharp Eye mutters words of a language I am unable to understand.

Wind blows in a stench and all is quiet save the sand that dances across my face. "Sharp Eye?"

"It's over, boy. Stay still."

His hand touches my thigh and grows hot where the wicked insect bit me. The heat increases and I begin to tremble.

"Stay still now!"

"I can't."

The pain is too much to bear and the poison must already be swimming fast inside me. I can no longer sense any touch.

"Stay with me now," Sharp Eye says, and my mind fades and everything goes numb and the world before me silences.

***

I wake under blankets to the sound of something sizzling and the smell of meat in the air. I touch my face and I can feel the contour of my nose and lips. From underneath the wool blanket I can see a firepit covered with a great slab of rock. On this flat rock, a mound of meat is cooking, its fat dancing.

Sharp Eye stirs at it with a stick and then samples a few bites, fumbling a few in his hands. "Hot, hot," he says, before gobbling them up like a lizard.

He looks across the fireplace toward me and sees me staring at him from under the blankets. He grins.

"Feels good to be alive, doesn't it, boy? Here, a present."

He tosses a corked glass vial across the firepit and it hits the sand next to my head. I pull the covers from my body and grab the glass container. It's filled with a yellow solution with pieces of translucent material inside.

"Quite the job to get that out of you."

I look down my body toward my leg that is now bandaged and throbbing slightly with pain, but I no longer have the queasy acidic feeling in my stomach that was there before I passed into darkness.

I get up and pocket the vial.

"Here, boy," Sharp Eye says, pointing to the sitting stone next to his with his stirring stick. "Have a seat now and get your filling. Lights up in four hours and we still have about a day's journey ahead to your new lordship."

I walk past a pit in the ground about the depth of half a man's length. Four chunks of meat perfectly balled. I stare at one of the balls. I can clearly see there is an eyeball staring back at me, surrounded in shards of bone, ligaments, and other forms of mystery meat.

"Are those the..."

"Yes, the ones we can't eat at least. Too much rad filth, you know. Little rascals put up a good fight while you were in the between world. Now come, sit. These here are okay."

I sit down next to Sharp Eye, who is stirring and bringing meat from the flame below to the edge of the stone that is cool. As I eat, I feel somewhat perplexed. How in the name of Poranda was he able to stop all those wild dogs? An old man like him without any weapon, an old man with his raspy breathing and sudden spells of fatigue seemed very much incapable of such a feat. Furthermore, those grotesque meatballs he made out of them. What the hell was that about? How did he do that? How did he suck the bug's venom from me?

There are so many questions, but hunger overtakes my curiosity and my will to get answers. I'm sure things will come to surface later. I just need to concentrate on getting to our destination, to Sara.

Sharp Eye pats my back. "It wasn't your fault back there, you know," he says. He looks at me; one of his eyes is foggy like Grangers Valley at dawn back home. He scrapes in more meat from the center that has finished cooking. "I'm sorry. I'm a bit short-tempered these days. Forgive an old grumpy man, will you?"

***

I wake up and our campground has been wiped bare. The firepit and the hole that contained the dead dog carcasses have seemed to vanish. The sound of footsteps behind me break the silence and Sharp Eye puts a heavy canteen into my hand.

"Over there," he says, pointing to the horizon to the east. There is a faint color of dark green. "Southeast swamps. Where we must go."

"How far is it?"

"We will be there before sundown. But easy," he says, pointing to the canteen, "that is all we have until we get there. Take it easy now, boy."

I nod in affirmative, and the thought of being able to see Sara again brings renewed energy to my mind and body.

We walk together, Sharp Eye and I, but I take the lead. My legs pump like a madman. Maybe we can make it to the swamps by midday. Sharp Eye falls behind and I grow irritated. Winds pick up.

I hear him yelling over the winds, "Slow down, boy!"

Slow down? I need to know if Sara is okay. Nothing is going to slow me down until she is in my arms again.

But the winds pick up again, tossing about sand. As I breathe, I can feel the coarse grit making its way through my garments and into my mouth. I begin to cough. I'm going to have a fit.

I drop to the ground and it feels like demons are trying to rip themselves from my lungs and crawl up through my throat.

My hands are painted in crimson, but this time it's different. Little specks of black sacks are dotted all over my hands and down my arms. I can usually recover, but this time my whole body feels like its burning and my head throbs as if it's wedged between two boulders.

Sharp Eye rolls me over as I gasp for air. He waves his hand over my face and down my chest and stops just below my rib cage. With two hands he rips my shirt open and slaps one hand on my chest in the same location.

He lifts his hand up and down. With each lift I feel as if I am going to throw up all my internal organs.

"What is this?" Sharp Eye says. He is yelling at the world as if he has failed at whatever he is doing. "I can't..."

I grab him by the arm and startle him at first, but he continues desperately with his pulling and tugging hand motions.

He looks into my eyes. "I got all the venom. But there is still something. What is this, Milan?"

My head drops and I stare into the blinding sun.

"My...curse."

CHAPTER 4
THE WAR WITH NO END

Thunder roars on the horizon and Captain Tygo's soldiers fight ahead, barely able to put a dent into Lord Deimos' army of drugged cave slaves.

Six days at this, six days of battling but a mere fraction of his armies has Tygo contemplating surrender. He has never given up once in his life, but this never-ending campaign against a psychotic ruler, a ruler that wants nothing else than to spread his dark hand across the Poranda continent, is testing his abilities as a leader.

They fight four sunsets from Forlorna and ten sunsets from the Land of Boulders where Deimos builds his armies and injects false hope of a new world into the minds of all that slip into his grasp.

Tygo has even heard from one of the POWs that there are talks of a special water that can be found in the ground and has great power, and that one day Lord Deimos will be able to harness it and further his grip on the world.

The pale volcanic gas-sucking minion said that Deimos is too busy with something to the north and that is why there is no necessity to advance west or south. The north is off limits, and even after three years of trying to penetrate his forces, it is clear to Tygo now that he will do anything to make sure it stays that way.

Each day he gets stronger. His cave slaves must be spending days in the bowels of the volcanos, because they are even madder and more reckless than ever.

It was on the third day that Captain Tygo knew something was different. He was face to face with what looked to be one of Deimos' cave leaders. He was about twice the size of the normal naked pale cave rat. This one had muscles like boulders, teeth like a Yala shark, and a face that could keep a man up late in their bed, haunted for days.

Though Tygo had hacked off both his arms with a bone scimitar, the brute still charged as if nothing happened, chomping at the air and pumping his legs forward. An arrow flew from behind, and Tygo watched as the brute was struck between the eyes. Even then the body twitched as if not yet accepting the path to the other world.

Captain Tygo's Lieutenant Maula marches forth from the back of the crowd of soldiers that continue forward, grinding the stone of war. Certainly, their bamboo armor will be sliced through and they will be gutted for meal by the northern cave worms. There just isn't enough time to train anymore.

But nevertheless, Deimos must be stopped. He plays with something that could bring about a fire to the world that can't be put out.

"Captain Tygo," Maula says, breathing hard through a bamboo shoot pierced in his nose. "The earth is black ahead. Fires spread and our troops burn as if the devil himself possesses them."

Captain Tygo catches Maula as he falls to a knee and is about to pass out. His bamboo vest has been ripped to shreds and something black has been smeared across his chest and his face. He reveals his hand covered in cloth and the skin has been flamed from the bone.

Out of all the years at war with Deimos, Tygo has never seen such an injury. It almost looks like a boar's foot that had been roasted too long on a firepit.

"My god," Tygo says, "These are burns, no?"

Maula nods, clenches his teeth, and covers the bony burnt mess back in the cloth. "Yes. But not just normal burns," he says. "When the fire was set ablaze by the spark of a cave slave, it was as if the flame wanted me. I could not put it out no matter what I did. It is as if the…"

Rock rains around them, taking around a dozen of Tygo's soldiers. Maula falls over on Captain Tygo. They roll on the ground and Tygo holds onto his faithful lieutenant in fear for his life. He doesn't want to lose any more men. This war has gone on too long and he loses a piece of his soul with each casualty.

"Maula," Captain Tygo says, and leans back so he can see Maula's face. But instead of seeing the Maula he knows, he stares into a bloody, pink concave that has been formed in the side of his head.

Tygo pushes the head aside but stays still underneath Maula's body. Rock rains again and screams penetrate the air. Bodies fall all around him and people are panting and puking and yelling.

Rocks come again and spray the back of Maula. More men fall and begin to cry out for help. A soldier falls next to Tygo and begins to mumble something, but when he opens his mouth, there are no teeth...and no tongue, for that matter. He has taken a mouthful.

Captain Tygo rolls from underneath Maula. He has never felt rage burn so hot on the inside. He has never lost so badly in all his years as captain of the Forlorn military. He has grown tired of losing and a sense of disparity spreads like a festering disease.

He charges forth, bone scimitar in hand, and is sucked into the crowds of men ahead that clash with one another. His men stab at the cave vermin with bone spears and slash with short swords. The swamps back in the south provide a great number of grass hogs and their bones now lunge forth. The bamboo forests provide the armor and shields.

They have the speed and tenacity needed to bring down the naked cavemen. Besides succumbing to the rock rain that had plummeted them, Captain Tygo begins to feel at ease now that his soldiers are pushing forward without much trouble.

It is just when Captain Tygo starts to feel his nerves calm that a new nightmare arrives at the gates of this never-ending nightmare.

He can feel it in his skin. Screams come from ahead; metal slices through bone, screams through air. Black smoke billows from where the sharp cries are born. Some of his soldiers are already retreating and running away, some even impaling themselves on spears as they try to disappear into the back of the defense unit.

From ahead he sees now what they fear. A caveman the size of a five-year-old Trusset tree pushes a wooden cart that carries a silver metal barrel. Two smaller cavemen sit in the back cranking some contraption as black liquid spits forth from a spout onto all that get in its path.

Men are drenched in the filth and set ablaze by archers shooting fire arrows. They try to roll around and put out the fires, but it's like what Maula said: it's as if the fire is alive and wants its victims.

His men burn before his eyes. He has lost.

Rocks rain again as he makes his way to the archer brigade. They whistle past his ears and one strikes an earlobe, ripping the bottom half off. He screams.

He orders the archer captain to focus on the great barrel that burns his armies, but the arrows that fly on his command do nothing as the great cave slave that pushes it is protected by a metal roof. The fire archers are also unscathed. They, too, are protected by metal shields as they slowly walk along the side of the cart.

Soldiers dwindle to nearly five percent of the original forces and Tygo falls on bended knee.

Hala, Tygo's archer brigade leader, grabs his arm and pulls him up. His eyes are wide and his teeth are black with Jasmin calm weed. "What are we to do now, Captain?"

There will be no survivors if he presses on.

"Make the call to retreat. Kill any that look to have a heartbeat."

"Our own too?"

Captain Tygo nods.

Hala takes up the horn and makes the call to retreat. He then blows a bone whistle four times to signal death rain.

It is worse than he thought. The rumors of this black liquid that stinks the earth are true. If this is just a small display of Deimos' great dark hand that plagues the north, then what more could be waiting?

A hawk cries from above and lands on the cart of supplies they pull back toward the direction of Forlorn fortress. It drops a message scroll on top of one of the crates and quickly takes to the skies.

One of the archers takes the scrolls into his hands and begins to unroll it.

"It says, 'The weird one will be at the swamp gates by nightfall.' What does it mean?"

Captain Tygo stares at the archer, the cart pullers, and the rest of the survivors and injured. "It means we need to hurry, men. I must speak with my brother."

CHAPTER 5
LORD DEIMOS

From his dome room atop the Shard, a black crumbling tower of steel and rock that sits snug next to Mt. Gray, Lord Deimos gazes upon the Gorgan Sea and sucks in salty air through his noseless face. He stares from his bone throne pointed toward the endless black vastness of the eastern horizon.

He has defeated her, conquered her, ruled her, and he will do the same to the bugs that scurry across the lands to the west. He will need the help of Poranda and the power of the black sauce in her womb. Only a few truly know the secrets of it. The one with the sick blood deep below in the rocks can only be tortured so much.

Deimos grips the bone arm of his chair and twists until it cracks. For some reason, today the sea boils his spirits as his eyes suck in the calm surf. There are too many memories in that black sea and on this day, and he remembers the disappointed face of his father as he came back to port after days on the high seas.

Deimos sits on the bow of a rowboat paddling toward the coast. It's so foggy he only knows the correct direction by the location of the faint disc of sun that burns behind overcast.

He has another boat tied to the one he paddles. The boats are filled with severed arms and legs stringing with flesh, eyeball-less wet heads, and a plethora of internal organs of various dark pinks and purples.

"Why just you?" Deimos' father says as he grabs his hand and pulls him to the Fishrat Village docks. "You were supposed to protect them. What did you do?"

Villagers begin to surround the docks. They mutter this and that right in front of him and shake their heads back and forth.

"Well?" Father asks and then backhands Deimos. He drops to a knee and flinches. The sting is easily forgotten as the sweet taste of warm blood fills his mouth. "We were to get a month's supply of grass flour for protecting the fishermen."

"The jumper sharks came too fast," Deimos says, and swallows the blood in his mouth. "The fishermen were too many, and too dumb."

Another hand comes and slashes the temple just behind his eye. Father begins to heave up and down and takes in deep breaths. "You will meet me in the basement before sundown. This is the third time, and you know what this means."

In Fishrat Village, people were given a warning for the first trouble caused, a humiliation for the second inconvenience, and a severe beating and seclusion for the third act of sin. It doesn't matter though to Deimos. He can take a beating like no other. Seclusion? He enjoys days at sea by himself, being swept along the coast in hollowed-out Gana trees. He will sleep the time away and dream.

"Boy."

"Yes."

Deimos follows his father as he limps across the dock and into the mess of wooden huts and stone pillars that make up Fishrat Village.

People throw stones at him and curse him. A wife of one of the fishermen bawls hunched over, burying her hands in the sand.

A young child pulls at his leg. "What happened to my daddy?"

"He's gone."

Yala Myan appears from behind a burn barrel with a trio of smaller kids, faces caked in mud and hair sun-bleached white.

"Oh, long nose, oh, long nose," Yala begins, making long pinching gestures from his nose. He is the worst of Deimos' bullies. It is never-ending and persistent. The other kids join in on the bullying.

One time, Yala pushed him on the ground and held his face on a rock and ordered one of his minions to smash a boulder down on it. Fortunately, the cretin tripped on a tree root and snapped his own ankle.

Yala continues the mocking gestures, but Deimos puts his anger in his pocket and continues to follow his father. There will be another day for Yala.

"Oh, no fun, Deimos dumb nose!"

Yala trips him and he falls nose first into black sea run-off foam that has accumulated on the beach.

"Bet that tastes great!" Yala roars with laughter. The kids laugh in unison while patting his back and tugging at his sleeves as if they want him to do more, mock more. "Run along to daddy now, run now, like the boar-nose monkey you are."

Despite the urge to snuff the life from Yala, he follows his father into the quiet of the village. They make their way to their box hut that stinks of summer mold. Father waves his finger over his shoulder to follow him down to the basement.

"Face the wall," Father says, and points to the other side of the muddy basement. Deimos goes as instructed and waits. He listens to the hammering of a stake and metal and then his father attaches a cold clamp to his leg.

"Do not look, boy."

But he looks anyway. His father unravels a long black cord about as thick as the village's fishing net rope. It's about five lengths of an arm.

He faces forward again, watching the wall, and wonders how long the pain will linger after the cord slaps and cuts into his skin. He is sure he can take it. He can take any physical pain.

His father's footsteps approach and he is much closer now, most likely making room for the backswing of the lasher.

"Son, you are absolutely worthless."

The lash comes. *CRACK.*

A line of pain from his shoulder blade down to the top of his left buttock stings like a mountain puna wasp bite.

"You and your weak blood. You and your ugly face."

CRACK.

Deimos can no longer feel the sting of the lash.

"Mutant nose, incompetent," he continues, and the lashes keep coming.

CRACK.

"Bad blood from your mother."

CRACK.

"Ugly born."

There are so many lines of searing pain across his back now he doesn't know where the new lashings strike.

But his father's words always strike straight to the heart, where it hurts the most.

"Ugly." *CRACK*

"Born." *CRACK*

Tears pour from his face. His heart is as dead as the fishermen, the ones who tasted his blade in exchange for spitting their vile mockery.

He hears the lashing come again, steps to the side, and rips the cord forward. His father is tossed toward him along with the black cord.

Deimos takes the hidden short blade from his trousers and lunges it into his father's heart.

There is no feeling, no shock as his father falls to the ground and the blade pulls from the hole in his chest. Nothing has felt more natural in his life.

Deimos then takes the blood-sweating blade and presses it up underneath his nose.

"Father," he says, gazing at the life pumping out from the wound in his father's chest. "No more mockery."

He pushes the blade up and begins to saw.

He feels no pain. Only freedom.

Deimos' mind wanders back to the now and the setting sun that spills an orange glittering blanket on the Gorgan Sea horizon.

He pets his father's skull, which is mounted on the left arm of his throne, facing out to the waters. A war brews out there in the world and there is no time for mind-wandering into the past. It is done and the future is now, it's waiting. All he has to do is reach out and grasp it.

Yala's stretched face skin on the wall next to the window stares back at him with its empty eyes. The people of this world have no souls, he thinks. He will bring them a new world and he will have all of Poranda under his thumb, all bent over with their backs breaking under his agenda.

Footsteps sound from behind. "The showers have started," his guard Puland says. "By morning we should have the newborns sorted."

"And Baya?"

"I have word he'll return from the southern push soon."

"Any word on the weird one?"

"Nothing, sir."

There is silence in the air save the loud crack from Deimos' hand that is gripped tight on top of his father's skull. Only the weird ones know where the baby of destruction sleeps. Only they have the secrets of the old world. There will be no new world without the help of the ancients.

General Baya had only one task. Kidnap the weird one from Tygo's band of swamp rats. If someone of Baya's stature can be played a fool and be defeated, the other cavemen will grow weak and unmotivated. He needs to show them that weakness is not acceptable and incompetence will be approached with unforgiveness.

"Puland, when Baya arrives, call him and the other newborns to the selection room."

"Baya has already arrived."

"Then go."

Puland bows.

"I won't be far behind."

***

Deimos walks beside the long conveyor chain rattling forward through the wet, dark tunnels of Mt. Gray. He loves the sulfur smells, darkness, and cavemen screams that come from beyond and echo along the walls. He loves the taste of their misery. Through their own suffering they are reborn.

A man is being dragged by the conveyor, his hand twisted and broken. His throat is blue and black with bruising. The poor soul must have choked himself to death. This happens. Sometimes Mt. Gray's fumes from below don't connect well with the cavemen's inner rage and they fear the shower more than ever. They would rather perish by themselves. This one will go to the shower but will never be a part of Deimos' great army. Weakness is a disease.

He enters the selection room, a black musty dome that glows under lamps. The sun has settled and it is cold and Deimos is not in the mood for failure. General Baya waits in the middle of the room, holding his leather clump of head protection in his hands. He stares at the ground.

He ignores Deimos as he comes into the room. His guard Puland makes his way to the north end of the room, where the chain conveyor continues to clink and clank and rattle its way to the shower.

Deimos approaches a fresh newborn, one who has inhaled Mt. Gray's innards and survived and is calm and strong. The caveman is not afraid to die. He almost looks to beg of it. And it is exactly what Lord Deimos of the north needs in his campaign. An army that doesn't fear the door to the afterlife.

Deimos nods to Puland and his guard unshackles the caveman and he falls into his arms. Puland hugs him and tells him that he loves him and that he will be the strongest of all the men that are rubbed hard under the hand of Deimos. Puland massages the pale, bald man's head, rubbing it in circles. He whispers the old religious words from a forgotten text and promises him glory in all things.

The next caveman appears and is conveyed along the wall. He is biting at his hand. Two of his teeth have buried deep in his flesh behind the shackle on his arm. His eyes are bloodshot and he tries ever so hard to release himself.

Deimos rubs his black claws along his cheeks as he passes by the room. So weak, so unworthy, but not worth killing with his own hands. He will let the shower take care of him like all the rest of the defects.

He turns to General Baya and it's almost impossible to control the tremors below his ribcage. His jaw muscles grow numb from all the teeth grinding. He feels as if he has almost lost the war and his will to move on.

He will not have failure again.

Puland brings in all the newborns who have made it through Deimos' mountain of transformation.

The room is full and the strong cavemen grin and their saliva hangs. They are hungry to serve, hungry to give their bodies to the cause of Lord Deimos.

Deimos brings his hand up toward General Baya and waves a long pale finger, a long black nail toward the white-faced failure.

He drags his feet forward and joins Deimos next to the chain conveyor.

"You have failed me, have you not?"

Baya nods.

"Do you know what this means?"

Baya looks down toward his feet.

He is a worm. A complete utter centipede from the cracks of hell.

There is a time for forgiveness and a time to teach. Weak people forgive and strong people teach. The more you forgive, the more you set yourself up for vulnerability. In the new age that Deimos brings to the world, there will only be strict teachings and obeisance. The new world will be perfection.

Before Baya can grip the situation, Deimos shackles the general's hand to the conveyor chain and follows him as he is dragged along the wall. Baya slips away from sight and into the next room.

He screams in a sloppy hot mess.

Deimos licks the wall up and down, tasting the sulfur and salty grains expanding in his mouth. He has never been so aroused.

The general burns. He gurgles. He is roasting alive and screaming as the lava from above pours onto him.

He sleeps while cradling unforgiving weakness.

CHAPTER 6
THE REUNION

When the world comes back to me, I am on a mess of wooden boards and rope, and I feel tugging on my stomach. Sharp Eye hovers over me, making long pulling motions from below my ribcage. With each pulling gesture, my innards feel like they're boiling.

I grab his hand and he stops.

"Whatever you have," Sharp Eye says, shaking his head back and forth in disappointment, "it's not good."

I am one of many born on the western coast of Poranda that has fallen to the invisible plague of the long-forgotten ancient world. Nobody knows where it originated except that it's deep in the ground, and if you are unlucky it will seep deep in your skin and rot you out.

"It's my curse, old man. There is nothing you can do."

He nods in affirmation as if he knows deeply about the thing that resides in me.

Sharp Eye lifts me to my feet and pours water over my head and then hands me a canteen.

"Drink."

He takes out a chunk of jerky and rips long shreds from the dried meat.

"Here. Eat."

"How long was I out?" I ask, and can feel the water enter my stomach. I'm so thirsty. I take the meat from his hand and tear into it like an animal. "Do you…"

Out of nowhere, I feel a great weight come upon my eyelids as the food slithers down my throat. Sharp Eye begins to wrap rope around his mid-section.

"Enough, boy. Sleep."

I lay back against the wooden board and let the weight of the world close my eyes.

"We'll be to Sara in no time."

"Is she all right?"

"That we will come to find out. Be patient. Rest. Your new master will want you fresh. He may not release Sara if you cannot serve him well."

"Who is this master?"

"Sleep," Sharp Eye says, and pulls me ahead through sand and dust.

***

I wake up in a great hall on a bundle of blankets. Three rows of dining tables rest in the middle and there is a podium on the far end of the room. The air is damp and smells of accumulated green froth brush in mid-summer.

Sharp Eye looks over me and points to the end of one of the tables. A chunk of meat and a variety of dark greens are slathered together on a white plate.

"Wake up. We made it."

My stomach no longer burns and I must admit, despite the growing hunger, I feel better than I have in the last six months.

"Where are we?"

"Forlorna Fortress. We are in the dining hall."

I remain silent, trying to dig deep in my mind, but nothing comes about. I have no clue of the place that I exist in.

"We are far to the east, in the swamps. It's the only place of civilization in these parts. Do you not know?"

I shake my head.

Sharp Eye sighs. Which is understandable. But my people of Bangal do not travel and believe in nothing more than keeping tight to the animals we raise as if they are our own sons and daughters.

I hear footsteps and talking from the distance.

Sharp Eye grabs my shoulder.

"Your lord," he says. "Your daughter."

I get up as if I am totally renewed from the episode in the desert and look toward the noise.

I cannot see the face of the man from the back of the hall, but I hear Sara's giggle and then she rushes out from the shadows.

"Father!" she yells and nearly knocks me over as I embrace her. Her hair and face are clean, and instead of the dirtied wool clothes of Bangal, she is dressed in a fine cloth of green and wears some type of woven bamboo plate across her chest.

"Did they hurt you?"

I hold her cheek in both my hands and expect them to be wet with her tears, but her face only plumps into a smile. She shakes her head.

"You were kidnapped."

She pushes my hands away.

"I wanted to come."

"What?"

Footsteps approach, and my brother Tygo stands behind Sara. He wears bamboo armor that has been damaged and blackened. His face droops and his eyes are dark with fatigue.

Sharp Eye points to Tygo. "Your new lord," he says, then backs away to sit at the dinner table.

"You," I say, and slowly get up. I push Sara to the side. My nerves are like lightning now, and I tremble and worry that I might explode and accidently get her involved with what I'm about to do.

I have been fooled. I have crossed a desert and almost died. I was worried to death and didn't sleep for days, for there was no information about Sara. She could have been dead and these buffoons sit here now calm.

I charge.

But before I can reach my brother, my legs crisscross by some invisible force and I tumble to the ground at his feet, nearly kissing the top of his bare foot.

I look up at my brother, at his solemn face.

"Let me explain," he says. "There is more to this than you imagine."

I turn to Sara. "What do you mean you wanted to come?"

Sara blushes. I can see she is trying to come up with an answer that won't dissatisfy me, but I want her to tell me the truth.

Tygo cuts in. "She wants adventure, brother. We were going to take her anyway, but she complied without hesitation. Are you going to deny her the chance to get life experience?"

"And what experience is that?" I say.

"Saving the world."

"What?"

Tygo explains it all. He explains to Sara first that he and I were separated at a young age and that sometimes brothers don't get along and have to be separated. He went with Father to the east to live here in Forlorna with his new woman. Dad died young of a wild dog attack while hunting. Tygo blamed himself, but I've always thought that Father got what he deserved. Why Tygo would be on the side of our cheating father and follow him is beyond me. It left the taste of bitter leaves in my mouth ever since.

After that, Tygo vowed to be a leader of Poranda's southeastern swamp lands and worked up the ranks to captain of the Forlorna army. He fights someone he calls Lord Deimos in ceaseless battle and grows tired. I have never heard this name in Bangal Village or in the northern fields of my home. Surely whoever he fights, it is but a local endeavor and has little to do with Sara and I.

"But why take Sara away from me? Why do you need us? Can you not just leave us in peace. And why Sharp Eye? How is he involved?"

Tygo sets his hand on my arm and rubs it up and down.

"There will be no peace. There will be no hiding. I took you both away 'cause I know that Deimos' great hand will crawl to the western ridge. Bangal will blaze in flame. Everything you know will be gone," he says, and gives a great sigh. "We will discuss Sharp Eye when the time is right, but not now."

He continues, "I need your help in the fight. I need Sara too. She is smarter than you think."

Smart or not, a warring region is no place for a girl. I shake my head. "No, we go back in the morning to Bangal Village where it is safe."

Tygo scoffs. "As usual, you do not care to listen. No place is safe."

I find it hard to believe my brother, who I have very little regard for.

"If you don't believe me, brother Milan, then maybe I know a few people who might get your attention, might open those eyeballs that cannot see straight and true."

Sara, Sharp Eye, and I follow Tygo across the dinner hall and out the back door. We cross through Forlorna deep into the woods and across hanging bridges that swing above stinking black swamp.

The swamp slowly fades to land and we no longer hear the burst of bubbles coming from its surface. In the distance there is a small building made from rock walls and bamboo roofing. On our left and right, soldiers are sitting on the ground, bloodied and blackened from recent battle. I understand now that they are queuing.

Tygo opens the double doors of the building.

"Welcome to the infirmary," he says, and they walk past bed after bed on both sides.

A soldier screams and grasps one of his legs that is a bloody bandaged stump. A man with a bleeding throat is puking blood into a pan that a caretaker holds. They are all bloody and screaming and half complete. They have been stripped of their humanity and they will need to start anew. Who could do such devilry?

I try to cover Sara's eyes as we pass through, but she is strong and my hand can't keep her curious eyes away from the carnage.

Tygo turns to me. "You see now what we are dealing with."

It's cruel, it's hideous. Yes, I believe this. But when we go out the back and see the bodies being loaded into boats and see ones that are full float out into the darkness of the swamps and trees, I see Mother.

When Ma died of the invisible disease inside her, the same one I have, we sent her down Hotancha River, out farther west, to be swept up in the great Banval Sea.

It's almost as if I see her out there now with the other bodies being carried away. My chest grows hot and the lump in my throat makes me feel as if I swallow a hard rock. I miss Ma so much.

I wipe my wool sleeve across my eyes and grab Tygo by the shoulder.

But before I can say anything, he pats my hand.

"It's okay, brother, we can do this together."

"Who is Deimos?"

There is a long silence and then Tygo shakes his head.

"A nightmare. Let us go to the barracks basement. We need to plan for the next stage."

I pull Sara into my side and nod my head.

She hugs my waist and buries her wet freckled face into me.
I won't lose her again.

CHAPTER 7
BLACK BLOOD HARVEST

Lord Deimos gazes down from his view port on the hundreds of cavemen working to the sound of a new civilization. Mt. Gray's fumes from deep in her womb keep them bustling like a nest of Yung bees as they carry barrels of her black blood away for the war, for the future.

But the pump machines that run on man labor are slow, and he has told Puland countless times that the ones who get the blood first are the ones who will survive the next millennium. He grows tired of faces that do not feel his regard for the crisis at hand and the passion in his heart.

Lord Deimos turns to his guard Puland and pulls him next to him so he can see below at the mind-stinging inefficiency at hand.

"Do you see this?"

Puland nods. His face grows pale and he no longer has the vibrant color of the traitor that came to him from Tygo's army but a year ago. He is like a ghost that is losing its connection with the world and would vanish with a whisper.

There are but ten barrels along the wall, and Deimos knows that it will not be enough to fuel another successful campaign. Tygo has grown smarter and recruits the swamp rats in groves. If the campaign fails, everything fails. He must capture the weird one, he must have Tygo down on bended knee.

Deimos points a shaking finger to the wall where the barrels are.

"Do you think that will bring us success? Do you think we can bring about a new world?"

"We need time, sir. The men and the pumps are fast, but the blood comes up slow."

"What of Mt. Gray's northern expansion?" They were supposed to be done with the excavation on the northern side. He had expected that side to be already up and running by this month's full moon.

"We lost a crew. The ground fell through at the site and they were buried alive."

"And when were you going to tell me of this?"

"Now."

Deimos cannot tolerate the words of failure any longer and he grabs Puland by the shoulders. He breathes heavy and the hot air from his noseless nasal passage blows Puland's hair about. Despite this he looks unshaken, and it's as if he has little interest in compensating for his failures.

"Puland. Look one more time. Look closely. Look out there."

Puland moves closer to the edge.

"Now, look at me." Why do they not show him gratitude? Why must they all look at him like that? That face of slight disgust. "Come to me."

Deimos points to his nose.

"I said come to me."

Puland shuffles slowly over to him and then suddenly weeps. He begins to lick Deimos' wet nasal passage, working his warm tongue around the edges and then the inside. Puland's tongue goes in and out and Deimos' blood rushes and his crotch tightens.

The last time he was kissed was by his mother, the night before she was raped and killed at a seaport town south of Fishrat Village. Father didn't do anything about it and continued to sleep with other women.

He tries to put memories aside and concentrates on the texture of Puland's tongue. The euphoria overwhelms his senses, but he knows he must make an example, and so he pushes the blubbering failure back from his grasp.

"We are trying to make a new world," Deimos says, and puts a hand on the back of Puland's cold, pale neck. "We cannot do it with Tygo in the south campaigning to keep this rotten world. He has the weird one and he knows he has the upper hand. Without the old man, the ancient vault remains buried. Someone else might get to it someday. Then what?"

"Then..."

"Then many will have to be punished."

"I'll always be by your si—" Puland begins, but before he can finish his sentence, Deimos throws him over the edge.

***

The cavemen pump at their wooden stations, spinning the great wheels and sucking up the black blood that lies deep in the ground. The barrels come at a pace of but one per day now. Deimos knows this will not be enough to fuel his campaign.

Only the weird ones that were birthed from the destruction of the old world know its secrets and how it brings inanimate beings to life, only they know where the relics of the ancient age are buried. Without them, there will be no conquering, no new age, no new world. He must find Tygo's weird one.

The one he has now in his grasp merely mumbles and stutters and his words make no sense. No matter how many pricks and burns, no matter how many stabs and tears, he simply stares out from the lead cage and repeats words of nonsense. Deimos knows he is planning an escape, but there will be no trickery or voodoo magic so long as the bars of metal remain where they are. He will keep him there as long as it takes, he will keep him there till the world is his and then dump the old stubborn bastard in the mouth of Mt. Gray.

As he passes the clinking and clanking stations, the cavemen bow and their mouths crack open to display meaningless smiles. Pitiful they do not truly understand the grave situation at hand and his deteriorating mental state.

Deimos approaches the station at the end of the row and sees that two cavemen are pulling up a barrel from the well that the wood pump fills.

They are cheering amongst each other and patting each other on the back as if they have come across blood rubies in the Huland sands.

"Dei... Dei..." one of the cavemen begins, but cannot finish the words and begins rubbing his jaw back and forth. He looks up and he is as pompous and unintelligent as the first day he walked into the Shard seeking refuge.

"Sorry, Lord Deimos," the other caveman says. "He is not taking well to Gray's breath today."

"I can see that."

"Dei... Dei..."

Deimos approaches the one who has taken in too much of Gray's offering and stutters now before him. He is worthless. No, *it* is worthless. Anyone who compromises the will of Deimos' hand shall be snuffed out. Anyone who doesn't believe in rigorous rules such as no breath of Gray while on pumping duty deserves no glory. There is no glory for him now.

Deimos nods to the one who follows the rules and believes in the will of his master. "You know what to do."

There is no hesitation. This one is strong. This one follows the rules and grabs the overdosed mess by the shoulders and jams his head into the great gears of the pump.

Deimos walks away as the crack of a skull splits the air and the incompetent caveman's brains moisten the air with a fine fragrance of fresh meat. There will be only order. No more mistakes.

He makes his way down the long corridors thinking of the cavemen, thinking of how they are so proud of how they bring up meager supplies of black blood. He grows impatient with everything. Maybe the relics will show him the way to the main source. Somewhere below there must rivers flowing and great reservoirs.

The chain conveyors are working double duty today and move along the walls with increasing speed. The new recruits are being dragged to freedom or shower in greater numbers. Meat and muscle are the only way to keep Deimos above the swamp rats, for now.

But it has been clear to him over the past days that it will take something special to get Tygo's weird one talking. It will take someone that could survive the end of the world again like his forefathers before him have.

It will take the Claw.

The chain conveyor stops.

Deimos stops at the wall and makes his way deep down past the bewildered recruits who are fixated to the chains that make way through Gray's bosom.

He must be ready. Surely by now, after weeks of preparation. Surely after being taken in from the very beginnings of the campaigns. Claw will perform the duty well and not fail as the cave slime before him have.

When Deimos passes around the corner and sees the hulking mass of Claw sitting on stone and taking well to Gray's fumes, he realizes that he might have a chance this time.

Claw's back heaves up and down as the cracks in the wall hiss out yellow fumes billowing across his pale gray bald sweating head. His body is thick with heavy lead plates but he gets up as if they weigh but a feather and turns to Deimos.

His eyes are yellow-shot after days down here sucking in the fumes. His hand raises. He wiggles his long razor nails like some horrific monster of the sea bottom and takes a nail to his tongue. With one swift motion, a dark purple mass falls to the floor.

Deimos sees that the man before him desires to prove himself a man of action and not words.

Admirable, Deimos thinks, but insufficient.

Like the rest of the ones that are under his thumb and suckle from the tit of the Shard, they must truly prove that they devote themselves wholly to the cause.

Deimos waves a bony tired hand to the center of his face.

"Show me," he says, closing his eyes and breathing in deep.

He waits for it.

Then it all comes forth.

The bloody stump dances inside his face. Claw gives himself to the cause. There will be no failure.

Never again.

CHAPTER 8
CLAW

The black waves of the Gorgan Sea slobber against the hull of Claw's boat as he makes his way south along the east coast of the Poranda continent. Dim lights from Fishrat Village now fade behind him. He digs his oars into the dark waters below deep and fast with very little interest in the shithole of a fishing village outpost that is the birthplace of his master.

He has a mission: Capture the weird one and bring him back to Lord Deimos alive. It is a mission that he is unable to fully accept in his heart. There will be no promises. The only thing that he can promise Lord Deimos is that he will follow his heart. He will do what needs to be done to come ahead in life. Weak die. Strong survive.

Yes, that is correct, he thinks. But betrayal, yes, this is what will truly save him. You are only the master until you are betrayed and put upon a pedestal among the masses naked and weak.

He needs to stay strong.

His oar bumps into something firm.

Black eyes emerge from the water and a mouth sinks into the side of the boat. Beasts abound everywhere in this cruel world. He must stay strong. No, strong is not enough. Cruel, yes, and unforgiving, and even relentless. Claw brings his fingers together, forming a spear of five razor nails, and plunges it down onto the shark's soft head.

The tail thrashes for a second but then the gray black-speckled body goes limp and the mouth full of bone shards gapes open.

Claw's stomach grumbles and he realizes now he hasn't had a meal in two days. Even the hits from his wool cloths drenched in Mt. Gray's fumes can't hide the fact he desires a meal.

He rolls the beast over so its white belly faces up. He slides a black razor from neck to asshole and licks his saliva-drenched mouth as a bubbling mass of purple giblets are birthed forth.

Mt. Gray knows how to bring a soul to ease with her delicious perfume and relinquish them of any fear and pain, but sometimes she is quite clueless to what a living being needs to survive. She knows the spiritual, but not the physical. She has very little regard to those who take her in deep to assuage away the demons. Claw needs to be careful.

He scoops up the warm mass and begins to stuff his mouth. Blood sacs pop between his teeth and he swallows. The warm liquids go down fast, and he finds that the more he eats, the greedier he gets.

There is nothing left in the body cavity and he goes for the eyes. They pop to perfection and he enjoys the comparatively sweeter taste than the bitter organs he had made a feast of.

The massive chunk of bone and half-eaten flesh sinks to the darkness and will provide a nice meal for the sea bottom feeders.

He rows on through darkness, a stomach full and a mind bloated in gluttony. The heavy weight of his master's mission is caked onto his spirit so thick he can barely keep his elbows from buckling as he digs the oars deep into the water.

Claw had thought about it for months. How would he vanquish the very master that took him in and made him a tool for the glory of his campaign?

He slaps his face and takes the wool cloth to his mouth and breathes in. His trembling arms and fingers settle and the rowing becomes a smooth song along the glass surface of the sea.

Mt. Gray's breath assuages all, and it's clear to Claw that he could sink and die and it would matter not. This is the power of Mt. Gray. All senses are numbed and all desires are sanded down to a blank nothingness. Take me deep, Claw thinks. Take me to the bottom. He breathes in the fragrance from the cloth again.

A metal hook attached to a rope drops into the boat and then rips tight to the inner wall.

He hears voices in the distances. High-pitched laughs of celebration, perhaps. From a misty wisp of fog, he sees a man winding in rope on some wooden contraption. He has a grass wrap snugged tight in the corner of his mouth and his arms crank and crank and crank until Claw is no more than three boat-lengths away.

"By the gods of grace, what do we have here?" The man cranking looks back toward a clump of crew sitting fixed in positions with thick pieces of wood and metal in hand. "Why, this one looks a little lost. God almighty, almost no loot. What of this one, Captain?"

Claw just waits as the front of his boat bumps into the Black Rust pirate's vessel. If he was weak and tender, full of fluff and ready to die, he would tell himself that he had gone too far to the east from the coast into the Black Rust island pirate colony. He would have torn skin from his scalp and sacrificed himself to the Shard mouths of the deep.

But now, with Mt. Gray's deep fumes running fast through his veins, he looks at the situation in front of him as an opportunity. He waits patiently. There is no need to rush as the star on the horizon still sleeps soundly.

Claw lets them capture him. He knew he would run into the Black Rust pirate company at some point, and there is no point in fighting yet.

"We got ourselves one hell of an ugly rat, Yalan."

They tie up Claw with fishing net. He doesn't mind. It's all exactly as planned. He insists that they keep him on their vessel that is more than four times the size of his Birk tree-trunk boat. It's all according to his will.

"Wrap him up good and tight now," Yalan says. He must be the captain of these sea scum. He has a black hat on in which the rim looks chewed and his eyes are bloodshot, redder than a rose and yellower than jungle Tree Trala shit.

"If he so much as squirms, send this into him."

He throws a dried Trintla carcass toward one of his crew. Even dead and sucked of all its juices, this black ball of a nightmare still retains its poison in its tail. One drop in your system sends you singing a tune to the end of all.

The deckman lifts the ball up above his head, tail end pointed down at Claw's head. But it's pointless.

His finger has already worked through the rope.

He already knows who will die when and where.

He could almost yawn.

He does yawn.

The sharp tail of the Trintla comes down and Claw takes the arm whole from the deckman. It gives a sad splash into the waters beside the boat. Other deckmen come, but they, too, lose limbs here, eyes there, crimson blood splattered everywhere.

Yalan rushes at Claw screaming with a scimitar but his eyes bulge when Claw's hand rips across his abdomen and his arms become heavy in his own intestines. He falls over the side of the boat and disappears into the waters.

Claw tries to speak, but there are only mumbles. He has no tongue. And that is fine. He loves this new way of life, keeping everything internal.

When he is master of the world, no one will be able to get any information from him. No matter how many times he is whipped, cut, or burned.

He kicks and flings the remains of the pirates into the dark waters. The surface comes to life and is disturbed by thrashing. Dinner is served to the twilight hunters.

Claw travels through the morning and enjoys the ease of his new sail. The coast is easy traveling now after passing the Black Rust cretin colony. Orange colors play among the ripples in the gentle water, and for the first time in a while, Claw's mind feels at ease.

He departs from the Black Rust vessel and makes his way to the beach. Just over the sand and in the distance, he can see a green maze of hot jungle.

Through the mess and stink of green he imagines the weird one waits. Never mind his master, who has taken him and brainwashed him. He still finds it hard to keep Deimos' voice out of his head.

It's always, "You are lucky I got you out from that shit cave village Yoolan when you had a chance. Your father was going to kill you."

Looking at the wounds on his arms and legs now from countless sufferings placed upon him by Deimos, he almost wishes that his own father had snuffed him out while he was still young.

Now he is by himself. Lord Deimos is no longer master of his life. He is far away to the north, and in time he will no longer be a memory in the minds of the Porandans.

Through the jungles, through it all, lies the weird one. There will be a new world. Deimos will no longer be the one holding thick rope skin of a beast and flailing it about to order those to his will.

"*Aw pilla gornat farl.*"

He knows that the words that come forth, stumbling over his stubbed tongue and crawling over his lips, make no sense. But in his mind, he knows one thing and one thing only: *Lord Deimos will die.*

Claw wipes Yalan's brains from his face and enters the swamps.

The Pater biters hate human blood.

But to Claw, blood is the only thing that wakes his spirits, the only thing that matters in this dull, dark world.

He sucks in Mt. Gray's breath, slings the lead vest across his back, and wades forth through the black swamp.

CHAPTER 9
A GIRL'S GAZE

The barracks basement is empty save the wooden table in the middle in which a trio of lamps hang overhead. Above the lamps, nets abound. Tygo says they are for the floods. They help people get out if the basement fills. He rushes ahead while I carry Sara. She seems tired but I tell her to stand strong and then let her down. She needs to hear the plan. She needs to know everything.

I grab my festering gut and see that Sharp Eye looks me up and down.

"I'm okay," I say, but his raised eyebrow and pursed lips imply something different. We gather around the table.

Tygo pulls a map out from a massive document filer of wood that is secured tight against the wall.

"Here we go," he says and begins to unfold the weathering scroll across the surface of the wooden table. The map says *Poranda*.

"We are here," Tygo says, pointing to the southeast of the continent. *Forlorna.* "To the far north, Lord Deimos and his drugged cave worms crawl like a disease under the skin."

Tygo eyes me and juts a finger at a tower. *The Shard.* "Here, Milan. This is where the plague of the world resides. If you think you and Sara are safe, you are oh so very wrong."

His finger glides across the map from northeast to southwest and his fingertip comes to a stop at Bangal Village.

"He already has troops just a couple days out from Bangal Village."

A nightmare this man is, my brother keeps saying, but it is hard to believe just a single individual could come to such power and reign over the Poranda continent.

I push the map aside.

"This is all nonsense, brother."

"Nonsense?"

"Yes, goddamn it, nonsense."

Tygo slaps my face.

"I brought you here because that demon out there will stop at nothing. Do you think this is a joke, mad man?"

I slap Tygo's face. I can no longer pretend that I don't care that he stole my daughter in the night and made me travel for days over desert for some stupid campaign.

Sara pulls at my trousers.

"Let us stop this, Father. I want to just have adventure; I just want to have fun. That is why I agreed to leave Bangal Village in the first place."

I smile and then take her red cheeks into my hands. She has a strong weathered face for her age, but there is much evil in this world that would snatch her up without a thought. I need to stay close to her, always.

"You are right. You are right about stopping this quarrel. But to adventure?"

Tygo cuts in.

"Girl. Adventure is a poor choice of word. This is a matter of life and death. The being we are up against intends to turn lands into ash and mothers into whores."

I give Tygo a hard eye at his choice of language, but he shrugs me off and continues.

"There are little mountain cavemen left. He intends to move west and take over the prairies and other farmlands. He will then move south and wipe out Bangal Village. You must see now why I pulled you from the warmth of your family life in the night. I needed to make my point clear that you needed to leave. Sure, I took extreme measures. Sure, I made you travel across the desert and almost made you die. But you are here now. Yes? You must know now that we deal with something that will not flinch to kill when a weakness is exposed. Do you see what I have tried to do? Do you see that I only want you and Sara safe?"

Tygo slams his hand down on the table and the room grows silent as ever.

There is nothing more I can say. If what my brother says is true, then I will believe him. But still, I want to know where we go from here.

"And so now what? You take us here, I almost die, and there is no sense of direction."

Sharp Eye slides an old wrinkled hand along the scroll and points southwest of *the Shard* and *Mt. Gray*. "Look here," he says. His face is as sharp and expressionless as a Yinkla eagle.

Tygo's eyes widen and he leans in close and tight against the table.

"This, my friends, right here. Southwest of the Shard. My brothers and my sisters say that something of value sleeps deep in the earth here. It is information on something from the ancient world that could bring our way of living to an end. It may even have information on the location of it."

Tygo's cheeks begin to shake and his eyes twitch.

"How long have you known this?"

"I have known this since I have had the capability to keep it in my head. It is passed along our kind like Hindra tree fruit candy. Our kind swear not to talk of the ancients, but considering the desperate times that we now face, we must reveal as much as we can, show as much as our minds will allow, and bring about a new method to finally vanquish this new evil from Poranda."

Tygo is breathing the air in hard and Sharp Eye tugs at his shoulder.

"It is too soon to feel disparity. We will win this. We will go to the underground lake, Bluesater, with a group of infantries and uncover the clues of the world-ending relics. Deimos will not have this world. We will not allow it."

Sharp Eye looks at me. "Are you following?"

"This is all very confusing." Ancient relics? Some kind of important thing from the past? "What are these old relics you speak of?"

"Machines from another time."

"Machines? Like some contraption? Like some tool like we use for harvesting roots?"

Sharp Eye sighs.

He moves his finger to the northwest section of the map to the illustration of the sun. "Yes, like some contraption. It is a contraption that can store the power of our blessed mother, our blessed star. One was cracked open many millennia ago and ended the world."

I am even more confused than before. It's almost unfathomable; if this were to be true, then why keep it a secret for all these thousands of years?

"Why such secrecy?"

Sharp Eye puts a hand on my shoulder. "Dear boy, this is not something that merely everyone can and should know."

"This Deimos wants it for himself?"

Tygo nods and puts a finger on Mt. Gray. "Somewhere deep down the mountain there, deep in the belly, Sharp Eye's brother, Kalamthra, is caged like an animal and most likely being tortured about the whereabouts. There is no telling how much longer he will be able to hold up."

Sara puts her hands around my waist. "So, what you are saying is once Deimos gets the weapon of destruction, he will have total control?"

"Yes," Tygo says. "Total domination of the lands. Total reign over the free will of all creatures that crawl on this continent."

"We must work together," Sharp Eye says, and begins to roll up the scroll. "We leave tomorrow to the underground lakes. We should all get going to bed."

I still have so many questions, but Sara looks up at me with sleepy eyes and pulls me down. "Together, Dad. We can do this together. Let's help them."

The door opens on the other side of the room and an old lady with a hunched back shuffles her way forward at the pace of falling tree sap. Her black cloak drags along the floor and she mumbles to some tune while chewing on a piece of brown Tyan wheat.

"Who are you?" Tygo yells, but the old lady keeps coming forth, her face totally covered in her filthy gray-white nest of hair.

Tygo's guards approach her. One of them puts a hand on the old lady's shoulder. "Old hag, this is not the time nor the place to be wandering about. Who are you?"

Tygo cuts in. "Take her away."

The guard turns his head in affirmation to Tygo's words, but in the next moment his head rolls down his abdomen and slaps the wooden floor with a wet smack.

The other guard tries to run away, but the old lady lunges her hand into the back of his neck and a cluster of black razor nails burst from his gaping mouth.

His eyeballs widen and he coughs crimson. The nails retract as he tips over like a fallen log to the floor.

As Captain Tygo charges the lady, sword in hand, I see her pull at her face to reveal her true identity. She is a man. His head is bald, pale, and appears clammy cold. His eyes are yellow with pinprick black pupils. They are almost demonic in nature. He carries a metal vest on his back as his free hand of shards dangles between his legs.

Tygo takes a handful of razor nails to the lower abdomen and is tossed against the wall. His head makes a thud sound on the wood floor when he drops and his body is limp at first, but his neck rotates and his eyes meet mine.

"Assassin. Deimos," he mutters, and then Sara is backhanded and her face smashes into the wall. She cries and crawls underneath a table on the far side of the room. She is angry and sad at the same time as she snuffles.

I feel her anger and I squeeze my fists so tight nearly all of my joints pop. No one touches my daughter. I will give my life for her and always be there for her no matter what slime of Poranda tries to take her away.

I grab the short blade from my inner pocket and thrust forth at the ugly yellow-eyed bald man that tries to end us, but he dodges every single try. The last lunge I nearly pop my shoulder out of the joint.

He elbows the hilt of my blade and I drop it to the floor. Before I can swing my arm around and try to punch the ugly mouth of the cretin, I get a mouthful of soft fabric and breathe in. It stinks of fermented root mash and sheep piss. I take it in deep against my will and almost suffocate from the smothering.

I feel nothing as I am tossed to the ceiling and rope wraps around my limbs. I tug and pull, but I am unable to free myself. All I can do is look down at the scene below, helpless and worthless. My poor Sara still shakes under the table, but she is now passed out and has fallen limp to the floor. I want to burn the world to get to her. I want to burn this whole place up and stick my knife into the pale man's neck where blood pumps hot.

Sharp Eye begins to wave his hands around as if to conjure something forth from another place, but the pale ugly one rips the vest from his back and lugs it onto him. Sharp Eye gasps and his hands and arms go limp against his sides.

Why doesn't he fight? I think, but then I see that he is petrified. He walks around in circles and tries to shrug off the vest full of clumps of gray rock, it seems, but he cannot budge it. He looks older and weaker than before.

Sharp Eye falls to his knees and looks up at the assassin.

"Take my head. Just do it quickly."

The assassin shakes his head and rubs his sweaty nose up and down the cheek of Sharp Eye and then sticks out a severed tongue from his mouth and grins. He begins to pull the chain toward the door and Sharp Eye is pulled forth behind him.

But like a lightning bolt from the heavens, Sara charges and jumps onto Sharp Eye. She pulls on Sharp Eye's arm, trying to pull him away from the assassin, but the chain tightens and the assassin's grip is too tight.

Sharp Eye looks into her eyes.

It is difficult for me to see everything. The fumes I sucked in have me seeing double vision, but I can see that Sharp Eye is sad and tears flow down his orange cheeks and into his white beard.

"You will be fine," he says, and his hand glows a neon orange for just a flash. Sara cries out and is thrown to the floor. She is holding her arm in pain.

Sharp Eye looks around as the assassin begins to drag him across the room.

"You all." His eyes are bloodshot red and he is sadder than the darkest parts of the night sky. "Take care. Yes. Protect each other."

Sharp Eye closes his eyes and folds his hands together. Flame bursts from his mouth and his body blackens.

Sara stares at the assassin.

The assassin can barely move at first.

Sara keeps her eyes intent on the beast of a man.

It's as if the tables have turned and the assassin is no longer a threat to her.

Sara's chest heaves up and down and her breath is raspy.

Yet, she gazes forward, and for the first time I see fear in the one that holds the burnt remains of Sharp Eye.

He flees as if a nightmare trails him close and firm.

That nightmare.

Is Sara.

CHAPTER 10
VISIONS

He won't escape me, Sara thinks. Not after what he has done to her father, Tygo, Sharp Eye, and the soldiers. His stink is easily detected over the Forlorna swamp steam.

The look on his beasty face when his eyes met hers stays to her mind firm. It was is if his widened eyes shot through a closed door to her secrets. Surely, he doesn't know. Nobody must know. If they did, she would be treated like a freak again. Just like she had been in Franshiq Bay, north of the Hotata fields, the place where she had grown up before her parents died, before Milan took her in. She misses them dearly.

She doesn't want to lose any more people. Milan is a loving father figure and now she has new friends. Nobody is going to take the ones she loves away again.

Sara wades through the swamp and sees the assassin disappear into a grove of forests on the horizon. She doesn't even look at the waters as the black biter worms swim at her with intent of an easy feed. Their presence vibrates on the tips of her fingers, and with a swift wave they coil and squirm and float to the mud bottom.

Her concentration ahead keeps the tongueless one strong in her conscious mind. She won't lose him. When she enters the forest, she can still see him through the thick foliage, huffing and puffing and sucking on a rag. He curses at the vines that pull at him and slow his pace.

The crunching noise underneath Sara's boots are welcome. She wants him to know that there will be no escape.

"Come out, you monster!" she yells.

The assassin groans loudly, but the words don't form properly on his stub for a tongue. He continues through the brush, slicing and dicing through with his long claws. His breathing is heavy and he sucks the air in long and hard. He puts a clump of wool to his mouth and sucks in even longer.

He begins to giggle uncontrollably, and over the next hours he tries to drown the forest in blood and fill Sara with fear.

One after the other, he slaughters the animals that inhabit the surrounding green. They come to his calls, a series of raspy grunts. The carnage of his claws spills the innards of innocence in every corner of the forest and Sara can barely keep her dinner down.

Sara continues forth, walking and swallowing. She will not allow the bile to intrude on her. There will be no fear from her. Even the whistle that comes and the sense that people approach from both sides now will not waver her stride forward.

She climbs a tree and continues to make her way forward, only a few paces away now from the murderer. All through the night, he stumbles over tree roots and bumps into the trunks of trees like some pathetic drunk.

Orange glow begins to spill throughout the canopy as dawn is on its way. The beings she had sensed throughout the night approach closer than ever, and she can now see in the distance tree limbs and other foliage that wave and crumple with their disturbance.

It's time, she thinks. Time to finish what she set out to do.

She moves ahead of the assassin, through the thick of branches and leaves, and then swivels around so that he will pass directly below her.

He doesn't see her coming.

The time is right.

The time is now.

She jumps.

Her feet strike the back of his vest and it splits apart from his body and drops to the forest floor.

He is totally naked now. All hers for the taking.

The ugly beast grins and leans back. He has given himself to her, and Sara calls upon her heart with anger and disgust as she raises her hands. She wants nothing more than to see this world without the stink of this foul creature in front of her and begins what the world wants her to do.

His arms retract into his body cavity and his eyes grow blank. Next the legs, and then the head.

She continues, holding all the forces strong in the air. She bites her lip, nearly splitting the skin open, and then screams as loud as she can.

The body crushes into a ball no bigger than her fist.

She screams louder.

Her arms shake, her body trembles, and her mind is in another world, another dimension.

The ball that is a man crushes and transforms even smaller.

It is now the size of a marble.

She leans over, totally drained of all energy, and picks up the glossy bead that is a strange mixture of crimson, brown, and black.

"Come out," she says, barely able to form words, she is so tired.

But the ones that followed her remain where they are, hidden in the thick of the forest green.

"Come out now. Or—"

Before she can finish the sentence, a pair of bald, pale white men shuffle out from the vegetation. They look similar to the assassin but smaller, their faces less disfigured and worn. They both go on bended knee.

Sara approaches the men.

"Deimos, correct? The one you serve?"

The man on the right bows his head slightly, and at the same time the other one nudges his shoulder.

Sara smiles.

She hands the marble to the one who is not satisfied with his partner's revealing ways.

"Take this to him."

The man takes it into his hand and gasps.

"Tell him that we are coming."

Before Sara can stop him, the other man slices his own throat with his thumbnail and falls to the ground.

She tries to interrogate the mind of the weakling before her, but he is as blank as a fresh blanket of snow in Bangal.

Sara turns to the other pale man who trembles at the sight of all the blood.

"Go now," she says, and he rushes ahead and the forest swallows him whole.

The open space is now but a dead zone with no sound, no smell, and no movement. Sara only feels warmth spread up and down her shoulder.

The sensation moves around her forearm like a snake and settles in a hot blazing coil that feels as if her skin melts and falls to the ground, burning in flame.

She drops to her knees, grasping her arm, and can barely keep her eyes open as the blinding pain digs deep.

Her mind grows white and then, like a flash through space and time, scenes paint her imagination like some great artist of a lost world:

Mushroom clouds.

Fire burning hot and furious and searing tree canopies.

People moving in great herds, their clothes ripped to filthy tatters.

Cultures and great contraptions being hidden.

Massive die-offs of humans and other animals and plants.

Deserts form and earth dries into cracked, lifeless terrain. Plains are sprawling and never-ending, fading into the horizon.

Sara falls to the ground and opens her eyes through the tree canopy.

There is another flash across her mind of a location under a lake, and then the vision finally comes to an end. She looks down at the black mark on her arm. The path is clear and there is much to say, and many to guide. Everyone must know.

"There is no time."

CHAPTER 11
SECRETS TO END A WORLD

It is late morning when Sara comes into town, dragging her feet along the wet stone paths that wind around the Forlorna bamboo tree forts.

Tygo's guards and I are just coming back from a five-hour search all throughout the night and I want to be mad, but the pale blank expression she makes before falling over sends a chill down my spine.

"Sara!" I yell.

I charge to where she is and skid to the ground where her head is buried in mud. Her face has plunged into a puddle, but she slowly pulls her head up onto dry ground. Black water streams down her face.

"Sorry, Daddy," she says.

"Hey," I say. She closes her eyes and her body doesn't move. She doesn't wake up. "Sara!"

She gasps for air and comes back to herself. "My arm hurts, Daddy."

"We are going now."

I scoop her in my arms and head to the infirmary.

Tygo is waiting at the entrance, his abdomen wrapped in blood-stained bandages.

"Quick now," he says. "Put her on a bed."

"There are no beds!"

The room is full of forty injured men from the previous battle. They all stare at us from the commotion.

There are too many people, and I have too many questions to ask my daughter, too many personal things. There could be more assassins or spies of Lord Deimos that seek information on what happened.

"We must talk in private!"

Tygo pulls my arm around. "Back to the barracks basement then!"

Sara kicks wildly in my arms.

"Not there, not there."

Of course. The barracks is where Sara saw Sharp Eye and Tygo's other guards get murdered by the assassin in the night. Her body shakes in my arms and she plunges her head into my chest as if looking for a place to hide.

"Come on then," Tygo grunts and limps ahead back out the front door and guides us to a tree hidden deep in the swamp forest. We go up the rotten stairs that wind around the tree trunk. I'm careful not to step too hard for fear of breaking through and falling below.

After a couple paces, we enter a wooden bamboo house squeezed between two hulking, ancient Hindra oak trees.

"My study," Tygo says. The room feels cramped. There is only a small wooden desk lined with an uncountable number of candles and a bed in the corner that could barely suit a grown man.

I set Sara on the bed. Tygo takes the desk chair and pulls it up beside us, gritting his teeth as he sits down and gazes at her.

He conjures a flask from under the bed. "Here. Make her drink."

I let her drink. I rub away her sweaty bangs and pet the top of her head in slow up and down repetitions.

She empties the flask in seconds and drops it to the floor.

Her eyes close, but she is breathing. And that's all that matters right now.

"Sara, what happened to your arm? You said something about your arm."

She mumbles.

"Can you show me your arm?"

I pull up her sleeve, and she winces in pain. Her forearm is a mess of blisters and burnt skin, but through the damage, I can make out the shape of a hexagon. A horizontal line and vertical line meet at a point in the center where a small hole has been created.

Tygo bends over Sara and as soon as his eyes meet her swollen forearm, he backs away quickly and puts a hand on the grip of his sword.

"Your daughter, she is..." Tygo begins to say, but he backs into the wall and remains silent.

"She is what? What is she?"

Tygo brings his gaze up slowly, but Sara is now sitting up in bed and anger spreads across her face. She gazes back at my brother.

"I am a freak."

"No," I say and try to put a hand on her knee to comfort her, but she quickly swats it away. I look back to Tygo. "What is this, brother? What is this emotion I cannot read? What has you so broken? Why is she so angry?"

"The mark, Milan," he says and sways the tip of his sword at Sara. "It is proof she is of the Weird One clan. Only their own kind can transfer such symbols from one to the other. Are you sure she is on our side?"

"What do you mean, Weird One clan?" This is all too ridiculous. Signs, who cares about signs. "What is this all about? Of course she is on our side!"

"She is of the ones that were affected by the destruction of the ancient world. The aftermath, the powers left after suns exploded on our planet, they all reside in her. The blood flows through her. She can do things."

I wonder about the assassin and how she chased him into the night without hesitation. I wonder about her powers. What powers? My mind rocks and I can't find and answer.

"What of the assassin?"

"I took care of him," Sara says, with no sign of emotion in the skin of her face.

These words.

That's all it took for me to back away from my curiosity. I had wondered how. But something about the mystery, something about not knowing felt right. Someday I would know, but not now.

"We need to leave in the morning," she simply says and falls back into the pillow.

Tygo gulps and then says, "The lakes?"

Sara nods and then closes her eyes. "He showed me where it is."

Where what is? I think, and then I remember Sharp Eye and Tygo talking about there being secrets hidden deep underneath Lake Bluesater to the north.

I can't bear to think of such hideous secrets buried there. I just want to make my daughter normal again and go back to Bangal Village.

Go back to my sheep and continue the simple life, but Tygo comes to my side and we both stare at a sleeping Sara.

"If Sharp Eye's brother is dead, then she is most likely the only one that can help us. Deimos' power grows too strong."

I nod, but I fear for Sara. I fear for her life and how maybe our world might never be the same.

***

Sara leads Tygo and me on horseback, and after a three-day journey northwest, we arrive at a broken-down wooden dock on Bluesater Lake. The area is empty save the small boat that nuzzles against the side of the dock.

She gets off her horse and waves us to follow. She leads as if she has been here before. But she hasn't. It's all Sharp Eye and the message map that he left inside of her.

There are two oars and a rope tied to a rock in the bottom of the boat. We board and I take up the oars in my hands. Tygo is still not fully healed from his cracked ribs and Sara is too small.

But Sara takes the oars from my hands and throws them overboard.

"We don't need the extra weight, Father."

"But how will we—" I begin, but I'm cut off by the sudden jolt of the boat. We float away from the dock and plunge into thick blankets of mist. Sara is at the helm, concentrating ahead, following the internal map from Sharp Eye. She looks to have aged many years since she first left Bangal but weeks ago.

After what seems like hours the boat comes to a slow stop.

Sara turns slowly to face us. "We are here."

"Tygo," I say, and look up and down his bandaged body, and he sighs.

"Yes, I can swim, Milan."

I throw the anchor over the boat and tie the rope tight so there is no drag.

Sara points to a part of the lake surface that bubbles and swirls. "Follow me, Father."

These are the last words from Sara above water. There is a splash, and she disappears into the black muddy waters.

"Follow me, Tygo."

I plunge into the depths after Sara.

The cold water hits me hard but it is not long before I see the blurry image of Sara swimming to the murky depth below as her feet kick up and down.

I think she disappears altogether, but see that she has gone into some square cutout on the bottom of the lake. Tygo bumps into me, and holding hands we both swim into the tunnel in the ground. The tunnel goes down for just a few seconds and then makes its way up. Our heads break the water.

"Come up here." I'm glad to hear Sara's voice as I pull Tygo up to the underground wet floor. Tygo gasps next to me, holding his bandages.

"Come on, Uncle Tygo. Need to be tough," Sara says and walks around the blackness of the newfound chamber.

"We made it," I say, and just as I wonder where in the heavens we have ended up, I hear a click and then feel a warm glow spread across the room.

It is the emptiest room I have ever seen, even emptier than my pathetic mud nest back in Bangal. A simple square room of mud. There is nothing on the walls save the sweaty compound of grays and browns and an indention that holds the fat grease lamp.

Tygo gets up to his feet and spits a clump of green to the muddy floor.

"Looks like this place is as dead as—" he says, but is cut off by the hand of Sara that slowly rises to tell us to silence our voices.

"It's here," she says. She seems reluctant. She rubs her arms and wipes her hands on her pants. "Father?"

"Yes," I say. "Are you okay?"

"Will you always love me no matter what happens?"

I go up to her and grab her arm. I bring her into my chest and wrap my arms around her. I push her back so she can see how serious I am.

"We do what we have to in life and that's that." I have heard enough from Tygo that I don't need to feel concerned about my daughter. She is special. I have felt in my heart strongly over the past days that she is strong. She is stronger than me, and anyone else for that matter. If there is anyone than can bring peace to the world, it will be her. It will be her that Deimos will have to face in the end.

"Please," I say. "Sara, you do what you have to do."

She nods.

"You are not a freak."

She caresses my hands and then moves to the center of the room. Both hands are spread out and her eyelids close. She is in some form of total trance.

Then, like magic from the realms of fantasy, a pyramid splits forth from the ground in front of us. Sara waves a hand and the top splits open and the triangular cover falls to the ground. We gather around this artifact, this thing that we do not understand.

But Sara doesn't look surprised nor fettered.

Everything in her composure is natural. It's as if this was meant to happen.

She takes the documents into her hand, and throughout the night our eyes gaze at the parchments and the history of a millennium ago. We learn things that should have remained buried. We learn that our world can end.

Everything points to the north.

That is where Deimos will go.

That is where the secret to the end of the world sleeps.

CHAPTER 12
VOICES FROM A CAGE

It dries out if not moistened or massaged properly on a regular basis. To kiss him is an honor, Lord Deimos thinks, and pushes away his new guard Ian back to his seat in the horse cart. He has done a fine job. His guard smiles, but Deimos knows that there will be failure somewhere and he will have to end him like the others and show the people he is a man that cannot be toyed with.

His armies have expanded far to the northwest. His hand is now past the wildlands and has already fingered the glacier field terrain even farther north. Thanks to the one in the box on the floor next to him.

A weird one who finally cracked, who finally gave in to the power of Mt. Gray's breath and the demonic blade of Deimos' will. There is nothing sharper than my will, he thinks. He gets what he wants, when he wants it and where he wants it. There is no exception, no other route.

"Lord Deimos," a cavalry man yells from outside and the cart comes to a stop. Another rider on horse approaches from behind, galloping like a madman through thick snow and blizzard wind.

Deimos watches from the opening in the cart as the man and horse come to a halt but a body's length away from him and his guard.

Steam blows from the beast's nostrils, and the scout atop his beast breathes in and out with just as much difficulty as his horse. He has traveled far, and this fact rubs a thick coating of curiosity upon Deimos' consciousness.

"What is it?" Deimos says plainly. If he so much as acts shocked or becomes emotional, he feels that even this could display weakness. The world he will create when he is done with it all will have none of that.

There will be no space, no room, no forgiveness for anything that isn't in the service of his hand that grips the Poranda continent.

"I'm thirsty."

"Shut up," Deimos says to Kalamthra. "If you want to live, you'll keep that ugly voodoo-spitting, infected mouth shut."

"But—"

Deimos kicks the cage and leaves the cart. Fresh air is needed and he could use a stretch after five hours of rocking in the cramped, foul-smelling space that the weird one has dirtied with his kind's stench.

The weird one, Kalamthra, laughs, but soon after Deimos exits the cart, he starts to sob and sniffle like a child.

Deimos clenches his fist and wants to bite his own tongue in half. When he goes back into the cart, he will teach old Kalamthra that weakness is a plague, he will instruct that one more outburst will surely solidify his own death.

But there is no time for this now. Deimos approaches the cavalry man and rests his hand firm on his shoulder.

"What is it? Tell me now, I have no time for trivialities."

"Lord, you will need to see this."

"See what? Are you dumb? You hold nothing."

"Lord..."

"Take more of my time and I will take more of your life."

The cavalry man gulps and puts out a trembling hand.

"But I do hold something. Here, look."

The man produces a ball.

Deimos snatches it. It is only the size of a marble and it looks like someone simply rolled up a ball of mud.

"What is this? Is this a joke?"

The cavalry man falls to a bended knee.

"It is the assassin, sir. Claw, sir."

Stupid cavalry man. He should have never brought them into the campaign. Stupid plain farmers from the wildlands that have less brains than a Hotata root worm.

"If this is some kind of play, then I would like you to bend over to me now so that I can remove your devolved dumb head."

"It is true."

Other men surround him and begin to nod their head. They yell, "He tells the truth." They are so sure of it, spit flies and nearly hits Deimos in the eye. That one is lucky.

Deimos wants to kill them all. They don't deserve to live. It means that Kalamthra will need to stay alive much longer. Much, much longer. Without him there is no chance of finding the relic. No chance of creating the world that has evolved in his mind for what seems like five millennia.

The cavalry man stands and his complexion is sharp and serious. He grabs the hilt of the sword and punches the center of his chest plate. "Lord Deimos. I have news about the weird one that follows Tygo. He is dead, sir."

The cavalry man smiles as if he has accomplished the feat himself.

Deimos will have them all slaughtered tomorrow when the sun first breaks the horizon. But now he has business to attend to. Kalamthra must cooperate. No matter what, the old beaten rag of an old fart must comply with everything from now.

Deimos' guard begins to laugh and swings his feet inside the horse cart.

"Oh, Deimos. It is going to be okay."

"Thirsty," Kalamthra cries from the cage.

"Deimos," the guard says, and stands. "Come in now and let's go."

The guard grabs Deimos' hand and pulls him into the cart.

"Those men are stupid," he continues. "We are going to make a world so right, so beautiful, so black, so grand."

Deimos pulls the guard so that he now stands next to the cage and his head hovers above it.

Kalamthra cries again. "I will die if I don't have water."

Deimos smiles.

The guard gives an attempt at smiling but his cheeks only twitch and it is an expression of disturbance and confusion.

"I'm dry too," Deimos says. "I'm so dry it hurts."

"Yes, Deimos. I'm sorry."

Deimos wishes that his nose being slathered and moisturized now would bring his heart to a state of stability and calm, but he feels more anxious than ever that Tygo's weird one has passed. Kalamthra is now the key. But what if he doesn't talk?

"Thirsty," the old weird one says again.

The cavalry man pulls his tongue from Deimos and kicks the cage.

"Shut up or you will get fed to—"

Deimos slides his thumb across the cavalry man's neck.

Crimson rains below into the bottom of Kalamthra's cage. The old man begins to lick at the puddle forming in front of him. He coughs at first, but then his drinking becomes thick and rhythmic.

Deimos tosses the cavalry man from the cabin. It's easy and no emotions nor reflections are required on the action that he has just taken.

He looks to the horizon and sees giant glaciers form on the land like great sparkling towers. A herd of cavemen are already chiseling away at the base of nearly a dozen ice spears that penetrate the clouds above.

"I keep you here now because I honor you for what you told me," Deimos says, bending down next to the cage as Kalamthra licks the floor where the puddle had been. "I respect you because of what you will give me."

The old man cries. It is clear he is breaking down due to the news of his brother.

"But give me more, Kalamthra. Give me more."

CHAPTER 13
THE END OF THE WORLD

The fog of war is on the horizon and we can hear the sound of marching as Sara, Tygo, and I make our slow approach to the fields of towering glaciers.

The word has been spread. Lord Deimos has found the relic of the past age that can bring this world to an end. I think of our lives, everything that we have known and loved, and check to make sure my sword has not fallen away to the ground as we ride forward.

I turn my head. Sara is awake sitting behind me squinting into the white foggy maze ahead. She seems too calm, too fine. She is not the girl I knew back in Bangal, she is something of another time, another kind. But no matter what, I will love her, I will protect her always. She is my daughter.

Tygo, on his horse, raises his sword and the blade catches the sun, and light dances in front of him. The blade falls down and an army of two hundred cavalry storm the first wave of Lord Deimos' cavemen that march through the fog in front of us.

Tygo's men have been healed, have been re-trained, have been told that their power alone will save the world, their honor to his cause will bring about a world of peace and maintain the status quo.

The cavalry men plow through the first wave of infantry. Their pale skin from many years underground in the darkness contrasts greatly against their open wounds that glisten with crimson under the fog-smothered sun disc that strains to send her rays to Earth.

I look behind me at Sara and she is watching with great interest. She begins to nudge my side with her hand.

"When are we going to do something?"

"We stay calm and steady until the time is right."

Sara sighs and taps her hands on the side of the horse. I know she is uneasy. I know she can probably do more, but for now, she stays with me. Before the thing inside me eats me up and my time's up, I will make sure that she is with me.

She yells, but I hush her.

She is strong, but there are times when you need to be wise.

The black blood comes and I make a dash past hundreds of cavalry men who charge and scream into the stink of splashing liquid. The smell almost makes me throw up along my horse's side, but I swallow and flex my chest.

Tygo is ahead of us, racing to the back. He shouts, "Ready the bows, they bring the black spreaders. We will burn if we can't stop them!"

And just as Tygo finishes his commands, black smoke billows and flames begin to devour Tygo's army. We will not last at this rate.

The head of a demon from old tales, the snout of a lizard breaks the fog and black pours out from its mouth in great vomits. Flame arrows ignite the men that have been drenched in the foul black liquid.

Sara and I race behind the archer team that is one hundred strong. Their bows point to the sky and bowstrings stretch with intensity.

Tygo brings his arm down and the arrows scream and whistle to the sky. There is silence as they take flight through gray cloud and billowing smoke, but not more than a couple seconds later we hear screams and we hear yelling. The cavemen that had manned the black vomit-spitting lizard beast are impaled by the onslaught and fall off the cart as it comes to a stop.

I see a sense of victory in Tygo's eyes. He rides his horse back and forth along the archer lines. He watches the slaughter which has been brought about by the rain of arrows and looks to be confident.

More carts from the fog come and continue their spitting.

Tygo looks flustered.

Sara and I remain well in the back as the arrows bite into the cavemen's pale skin and puts them into an eternal sleep.

"Use them all, men," Tygo yells as he makes runs along the front of the archer line. "Three arrows per shot!"

The skies turn black with arrows and the new carts that Deimos sends forth are barely able to touch Tygo's cavalry. The arrows are too fast, too many, and too unforgiving.

Tygo approaches us from behind.

"Are you two okay?" His horse circles us as if trying to keep away any vermin of Deimos' army that might have gone astray.

"We are okay."

"Sara, are you okay?"

"I'm okay," she says and gives a great sigh. "I would be better if I could help. The cavalry will not hold up much longer."

Tygo laughs and pats Sara's head. "I need you to be with my brother. Right here, right now. Your time will come. Soon enough. Be patient."

Tygo smiles. His face is covered in dirt and sweat pours down his cheeks. His helmet is dented where arrows couldn't penetrate and bamboo from his chest armor hangs all over his body. He is a true warrior; he is a fighter. And it's as if I no longer have any sour taste in my mouth about him moving away with Father out east.

Everyone has their own path in life and their own destiny to control. If you can't control your destiny, you can't write your own chapter.

My brother is brave, but my brother is too brave, and a shadow lurks on the horizon. A figure hides among the fog. He is tall, noseless, and wears a helmet of horns and armor that is sprawled in a metal wire mesh of black stones.

"Deimos," Tygo says and faces the silhouette of the man, the phantom. "Demon!" He screams at the top of his lungs and charges ahead.

"No, Tygo, no!" I yell at him. He must not notice the carts rolling ahead next to Lord Deimos. I shiver thinking that this is the man that wishes to threaten the world with old relics and conquer all.

I begin to cry. My brother doesn't see the pointlessness of his action. He is drunk with rage, drunk in stupor. His bravery is his weakness, and that weakness is a means to his end. I can barely breathe.

Black blood hammers into Tygo's chest. The black keeps coming, spraying him across the face and all over the horse he rides. He is drenched, but yet, he screams and keeps his sword pointing directly at Lord Deimos.

He lunges backward as an arrow penetrates his neck. His body roars in flame and his skin blackens. He screams, but the arrows wedged deep in his skin transform it into something of despair, something of pity. My heart sinks to the bottom of my feet. Sara squeezes me as we watch on.

Tygo finally becomes limp, his body charcoal. The horse still struggles, but it, too, is in a blanket of flame that cannot be taken off. It falls on its side, crushing Tygo. They both lay still, and they both come to their ends.

The last time I cried was when mother's head rolled along my forearm as I held her, as she closed her eyes and died from the same demons I have.

I get the same feeling now.

I'm so empty, so done.

I don't know if I can continue.

Sara grabs the reins and begins to wave her hands up and down so that the leather straps signal to our horse that we must gallop, we must charge. And that is what we do. I don't stop my daughter. She is special.

She will do what needs to be done. I trust her.

Lord Deimos stands just a few strides in front of us as our horse splits through the air and sends slobber in all directions.

I feel myself lifted and carried. The horse by itself gallops ahead.

Deimos stands tall with his blade, and four caveman the size of four-year-old Pinia trees tower in front of him. Their arms are bulky and they have blades fixed that glimmer in the sun that can barely smile warmth through the overcast.

The horse is killed.

A blade slices its throat. Other blades stab behind the shoulder blade. They are ferocious and vicious in their ways. So many strikes and attacks bring the beast to a stop and it falls over.

Black envelops the beast and it, like Tygo and his horse, roars in flame and becomes but a forgotten black smoking mass on the glacier fields.

I feel hands wrapped around my waist.

"It's okay, Father," Sara says. We float slowly down and my feet press against the field gently, my boots burying deep into the powdered snow.

"Let me take care of this."

"I am your father. I take care of you."

Sara stares at my chest, but then the grunts and the calls of the cavemen that are taller than Deimos come forth.

I try to push Sara behind me but she dodges my arms and rushes ahead.

Deimos yells something but I can't make out what he says.

Cavemen muscles rush forth with blades and the stink of their breath. I could smell them before we even saw Deimos through thick cloud and white mist.

Deimos. This name—this thing that has hovered among many and struck fear in millions is tiring my heart.

My thoughts mean nothing. My daughter is an angel of death. The moment I think she is about to get killed, I see an arm of a caveman crack and crumble and strike forth against the other cavemen that try to end us now.

"Are you okay?" I ask my daughter.

She rolls her eyes back and sighs. She says, "Father, please stay behind, please be safe."

That is my line, I think and trudge forward to the commotion that has been triggered forth and mixed in a cauldron of craziness.

Sara flies ahead of me. She jumps, but as she cuts through the air, a vest falls on her and wraps her tight.

When she falls to the ground whimpering and crying, the men surround her with spears held high, ready to pierce downward. Behind the men, Deimos opens his mouth wide and licks his lips.

The spears come forth but the tips break off and fly back at the cavemen. Throats are slit, eyes rip open, and limbs are rendered unfunctional due to the blast of metal and wood shrapnel.

I try to swallow the air, but the death that spreads around me clouds any form of judgment.

Sara pushes me to the ground.

"Father," she says. "You always wondered, always dreamed how the world will end. You thought that you would lose me. But I want you to know now."

She cries. She can barely keep herself together.

"What is it?"

"I want you to know that you will be gone soon. But I will take care of you. No matter what."

"I love you." This is all I can say. I am going to be dead soon, my daughter says. I will leave her soon and it will be her and the world.

I want to kill the disease that is in me. I am too close to the end. There is only my daughter.

She fixes her gaze on Deimos, the mad being that will try to keep all the secrets of destruction and renewal to himself.

He yells at the top of his lungs.

It's all slow motion from here.

Sara rips her arms forward and the dead cavemen fly and smash into Deimos. Their bones break and grind and spray crimson along the ground.

Deimos is at the center of the meatball.

We approach the mass of meat as I follow her, as she keeps her arms up firm and her body trembles.

She is so strong.

There is nothing that could wipe her away.

It would take the night sky and all its stars to push her away.

Most epic tales of heroism require some form of pinch that is almost impossible to get out of until the main character receives or finds out about some key item.

But that's not the case in Sara's story.

She ends everything swiftly and with a force that shakes the very ground where arms, legs, and ripped skulls pile in one bloody mass. I can't even make out who is who and what belongs where, but I'm certain that the noseless head that lies on top of the mass and stares up at the overcast sky belongs to a man who wanted too much in his life.

With Tygo's backup infantry, archery men, and cavalry marching ahead strong and with much more strength now that Deimos has been taken out, we slice and rip into their frontline efforts.

By sundown there are no more cavemen alive, and we make it to the base of a giant glacier. There is a cage that holds a frozen old man. He's bent over in internal sleep, but there is no time to wonder about it. We spend half the night passing through a maze of glimmering ice walls and damp rock.

Sara takes us deep and deeper. She huffs and puffs steam as she works hard to find the next path. It's as if she's afraid she might lose something important in her head. It's as if she will lose all the images Sharp Eye left.

The passage opens into a large room that has been hollowed out. Icicles the size of horses sweat down on us from above and snow no more than a pinky length crunches under our feet as we make our way to the middle.

Sara closes her eyes and looks around at the ground and then shifts her attention to a small rock. She waves a hand and the rock rises, bringing along with it a long shaft that slides up for a second but then slams down with a clank against the rock.

The rock wall in front of us comes to life and sinks into the ground, rock scraping and metal clanking.

An archive? A library of some sort? But why here?

Shelves upon shelves of scrolls and other books. The scriptures and writings are stacked so high there are ladders on every wall to make it easy to grab any part of the archive.

Sara waves the infantry away.

"Father and I only," she says. "It could be dangerous."

Some of the men give a long sigh as if their journey deep into the ground was for nothing, but the ground rumbles under their feet and they disappear back into the maze.

Over the next days, we are totally entranced. Our eyes sweep across the texts of hidden histories. We read about the fall of empires and the rise of moving contraptions and suns exploding on soil that nearly bring death to mankind. It is the history of *Earth*, the history of here, Poranda, before it was all destroyed.

My chest swells and I burn all throughout my body. I sit down and lean my head back in the rocking chair. But then like some sleeping volcano coming to life, I go into a coughing fit. I pull my hand away and it is wet and warm with my own blood.

Sara's hand caresses my chest. Her eyes are closed and she is silent. I feel the same tug as when Sharp Eye tried to heal me in the desert. I feel the demon inside me rise, but it quickly swims deep below and the great weight of its burden fills me with despair.

Sara grits her teeth and tears pour down her freckled cheeks.

"Father."

I grab her hand.

"Father."

"Knowledge is a weapon," I say and rub her cheeks and tell her that everything will be okay. I tell her why the archive must stay closed and why she must protect it.

I tell her she will go back to Bangal and then Forlorna and the rest of the lands and begin to rebuild. Only someone as pure as her, as special as her, can bring light back to this dark dream we live in.

My chest burns with a hot fire and my breath is sucked from my body. My head feels light and my world begins to brighten and my body warms.

The last thing I see is my daughter's face.

The last thing I feel is hope.

ABOUT THE AUTHOR

BENJAMIN DEHAAN is a speculative fiction writer and illustrator. He was born and raised in southern Wisconsin, USA, and now lives and works in Japan. His short fiction can be found in various magazines/anthologies, and his debut horror novella *Dust and Deliverance* was recently released from PsychoToxin Press. More info at his website benjamindehaan.com.

www.ingramcontent.com/pod-product-compliance
Lightning Source LLC
Chambersburg PA
CBHW030357180626
46812CB00007B/2920